Okei-san

A Girl's Journey, Japan to California, 1868-1871

by Joan Barton Barsotti

Illustrated by Alpen Kelley

Okei-san: A Girl's Journey, Japan to California, 1868-1871

Barsotti, Joan Barton
Okei-san: A Girl's Journey, Japan to California, 1868-1871
Illustrations by Alpen Kelley

Library of Congress Control Number:
Available upon written request to the publisher, Barsotti Books

Summary: In 1869, following a civil war in Japan, a group of people come to California to establish a tea and silk colony. Troubles follow success, and the leader returns to Japan leaving the rest of the colonists behind. This is the story of a Japanese girl's courage and pioneer spirit.

1. Emigrants from Japan to America – Historical Fiction
2. California Immigration – Historical Fiction

I. Kelley, Alpen, ill.
II. Title: *Okei-san: A Girl's Journey, Japan to California, 1868-1871*

ISBN-13: 978-0-9818188-4-9

Published by
Barsotti Books
2239 Hidden Valley Lane
Camino, CA 95709-9722
www.barsottibooks.com

Illustrated by
Alpen Design
Hornby Island, BC V0R 1Z0
www.alpenkelley.com

10 9 8 7 6 5 4 3 2

Printed and bound in Shanghai, China.

In Memory of

Carl Borelli
Carol Mathis
Emmy Lou Word

A Dedication To Our Mom

Joan Barton Barsotti *was a gifted writer and storyteller. More importantly to us - she will always be remembered as an irreplaceable mother, grandmother and friend. She passed way suddenly, in late August of 2010. She was witty, kind, generous, funny, vivacious and incredibly creative. She has had, and will continue to have, a profoundly positive impact on everyone she's met.*

If you didn't have the chance to meet her in person – of hearing her read one of her books, or sharing the joys of writing and publishing – then perhaps you can at least get a feel for what she was like in reading this book. She loved researching and writing this story. She wanted to bring this true story to life, and that's exactly what she did.

Joan Barton Barsotti
October 22, 1939 — August 29, 2010

She was the type of person you always enjoyed seeing, you wanted to run into her. You wanted to be seated next to her at special occasions or events, because she was so easy to talk to, and a good listener. She could keep small children busy for hours with creative games (from reading short stories to decorating home-made gingerbread houses), she'd engage teenagers in conversation easily and she could, without complaint, talk to adults of any age – having genuine, meaningful conversations. She could

dance. She could scuba dive. She would sing opera – loudly (but she really couldn't sing). She could play the bagpipes (badly – per her instructor, after six months of lessons). She could draw, write and sew. She didn't really like to cook – but she made the best cheesecake, Kansas city brisket and chocolate decadence you'd ever taste. She did all of these things because she enjoyed trying new things – especially if they were with friends and family – whether she was good at them or not. It wasn't about being good at something - it was about spending time with friends, being creative and making people feel good. She made life-long friends in an instant. And she always put other people's needs in front of her own. When one single individual has this much positive impact on so many others – it's worth sharing her life, especially now, with others.

We hope you enjoy reading this book as much as our mom enjoyed researching and writing it…just for you. It is, after all, the story of one girl who went on an amazing journey –not even knowing the significance it would have.

With love, from us all (Karen, Mike, Nick, Matt, Lindsay, Cathy, Matt, Michael, Mindy, Mark and Mia)

Table of Contents

Chapter One

Okei and Family, Wakamatsu, Japan, September 1868

Okei walked steadily along the road, her *geta* (wooden clogs) making a dull click-clicking sound on the dirt. It was early morning, sun rising, quiet. She liked this time of day. She would be at the marketplace within the hour, before the road swelled with people. The baskets she carried were heavy with produce, but she did not feel the weight of them. Although slight of body, she was quite strong.

Boom! Boom! Boom! She faltered for just a moment – sounds of gunshots, coming from inside the castle walls. She knew the samurai were just practicing, they were always practicing, but still she did not like this constant reminder of war.

She arrived at the marketplace and made her way to Uncle Haru's display table. At first he did not notice she was there. He was staring at the daimyo's castle, which stood so tall it looked like a mountain in the middle of town. Then his head seemed to fall forward, his tightly clenched fists relaxed and hung loosely at his sides, color returning slowly. He sighed, turned around and saw Okei. He did not smile. He did not appear to be happy today.

"Ah, Okei-chan. *Ohayo gozaimasu*" (good morning).

She bowed low. "*Ohayo gozaimasu*, Haru-san. See what I have brought for you today." She hoped the fresh produce would please him.

But Uncle Haru did not see the beautiful apples, radishes,

and cucumbers. Instead he picked up one of his own baskets and slammed it onto the wooden table. Okei jerked her head up in surprise. Uncle Haru never showed anger!

"Herr Schnell is going to America!" he said abruptly.

Okei knew very well whom he was talking about. Herr Schnell was the Dutchman. He had sold weapons to Lord Matsudaira, the daimyo, for many years and was his confidant. Herr Schnell had also earned the right to be samurai.

Uncle Haru took some apples out of Okei's basket and placed them in the basket on the table; then he just stood there not moving at all. Finally he said to no one in particular, "Herr Schnell is taking his family to America. He should stay in Japan and help fight the war that is here!"

The potter at the next table must have heard Uncle, for he spoke up hurriedly, "And soon the Chosu and Satsuma soldiers, the imperial forces, will come here to Wakamatsu."

Uncle waved his arms wildly. "Those southern samurai call themselves imperial forces? Pah! They are nothing but rebels! They want to take over the country – and Herr Schnell is running away!"

Now the potter began to raise his voice, and he did not agree. "I think Herr Schnell will stay here. He is still training with the daimyo's samurai. Even now he is teaching them how to use the new weapons."

"No," said Uncle Haru. "He should be here when the rebels come, but he is going to America instead!"

"He would not do that," said the potter. "He will stay here and fight, side by side, with other Aizu samurai. He is honorable."

Finally both men seemed to remember business. Uncle Haru took the radishes from Okei and placed them near the apples on the table. She had never seen him so angry.

"Haru-san, why is Herr Schnell going to America?" she asked.

"Because he and his family will die if they stay here," her uncle answered tersely. "He is not Japanese, but he is the daimyo's confidant. Many people have left town because of this war, but Herr Schnell is samurai and he should not leave!"

Then Uncle Haru's shoulders slumped, energy seeming to escape from his body. He sighed deeply. He looked at Okei and she saw sadness come into his eyes. She wondered if he was thinking of his son who was training with the daimyo's samurai. Both of her brothers were training with them also. Her father always spoke of his sons with pride. *Uncle Haru is fearful of danger,* she thought, and she was puzzled for she had never seen fear in her father's eyes.

"Okei-chan," said Uncle Haru, "the decision is not ours to make. We must go to the castle if fighting comes here." He glanced quickly at the daimyo's castle, and then he looked at Okei, worry showing deeply in his eyes. "What will happen then? We cannot stay there forever. Chosu and Satsuma soldiers need only wait until we starve."

The war between Tokugawa clans of the north and Chosu/Satsuma clans of the south had recently shifted in favor of the southern clans. The Tokugawa family had ruled Japan for more than two hundred and fifty years. Now southern forces were moving steadily north, seizing castle after castle and coming toward Aizu, where the last Tokugawa castle stood in the town of Wakamatsu.

Uncle Haru sighed again and Okei knew he was finished talking to her. He became busy with customers. She listened to them as they talked back and forth, sometimes speaking in hushed tones but mostly with loud voices.

"Herr Schnell is going to America?"

"Yes! Yes! He is taking tea growers, gardeners, carpenters, and samurai. He is going to start a tea and silk colony in America!"

"I hear he is taking his wife Jou and their daughter Frances. Why is he going there?"

"The daimyo is sending him!"

"Why would Lord Matsudaira send him to America? Does he think we will lose the war?"

"*Hai!* Maybe he plans to go to America, too?"

Okei was so interested in what they were saying that she could hardly wait to tell her parents. Herr Schnell, the handsome Dutchman who was married to a Japanese samurai's daughter, was going to America! She wondered what it would be like to live in America. She had never traveled any distance from home and did not think she would like to live far away from family.

She also did not want to believe what Uncle Haru said about the fighting. She knew everyone was preparing for war, even boys younger than her own sixteen years, but she did not think fighting would actually come to Wakamatsu.

Okei stared at the castle. *If Chosu and Satsuma soldiers do come to Wakamatsu,* she thought, *we should be safe there.* The walls were thick and tall and made of stone. A deep moat surrounded the castle. The daimyo's samurai would defeat the imperial soldiers before they could even reach the walls. She believed this to be true. The Aizu samurai were the bravest of all samurai!

— Chapter Two —

Bad News,
September 1868

Okei was glad when Uncle Haru told her she could leave. She hurried away from the marketplace, running swiftly along the road. If Mother could see her, she would not be happy. It was not proper for her to run like a chicken, but Okei was anxious to get home as soon as possible.

She was still thinking about Uncle Haru as she rushed into her yard. *I cannot wait to tell Father what I heard at the marketplace!*

She stopped under the big *keyaki* tree, the one that was planted the year her great-grandfather was born. She could hear the birds singing in the tree, always there, always happy. Her heart was pounding and it felt good to stay in the shade for a moment. She took the gourd hanging near the large crock and filled it with water, savoring the cool mountain freshness as she drank. She rinsed the gourd and hung it back on the hook.

It was hot today. The end of summer always brought the hottest days, and this year it also brought the war closer to town. Sometimes she could see smoke in the distance, a sign of fighting. Sometimes she was terrified of war but once inside her house she would not worry. Father never allowed outside troubles to enter their home.

She climbed the few steps to the porch, slid the door open, and stepped inside. She slipped out of her *geta*, leaving them next to Mother's. Even though she did not see Father's *zori* (sandals) she knew he would be home soon because Mother was busy preparing the meal.

"*Tadaima!*" (I'm home) she said, expecting the usual warm welcome, but when Mother looked up Okei saw tears instead of a smile. "What is it, Mother? Is something wrong?"

Mother just bowed her head and turned away. Her sorrow was so profound that Okei was frightened. *Is Father hurt? He should be home by now. Where is he?* Chills ran through her body. She stared at Mother. Why was she so sad?

The door slid open and Okei looked up as Father entered the house. He slipped out of his *zori*, walked toward Mother, and stopped. He looked old, older than Okei thought he could ever be, and she knew trouble had finally invaded their home.

At first Father did not say anything. He motioned for Mother and Okei to come to the table. Okei knew he would not speak until they finished their meal – the rule was no unpleasantness while eating – so she tried to be very patient.

She kneeled at the table, cupped the bowl of *misoshiru* in her hands and sipped the hot soup slowly; then she picked up her chopsticks and took some rice. She managed to eat the small pieces of fish and the pickles, too, but tasted nothing. Okei could not imagine what the bad news might be. She shivered with fear – her brothers? She prayed silently, *Please, let no harm come to my brothers.*

When they finished eating, Okei cleared the table. She was nervous and almost dropped a dish. How could her parents be so calm? She washed the bowls and chopsticks and put them on the shelf while her parents sipped their tea. There was no food left over. Mother always prepared just the right amount for each of them.

Finally Father was ready to talk. Okei returned to the table, impatient to hear him speak, but not wanting to hear his words. Mother was quiet, kneeling at the table, looking down at her tightly clenched hands.

When Father spoke, his voice trembled. "Okei-chan, Matsu came to see me today and we talked for a long time."

Matsu, a samurai, was her older brother's friend, and he was assigned to guard the Schnell family. Why would he talk to her father?

Father continued, "Herr Schnell is going to America and he is taking his family and Matsu with him."

"Oh, yes, Father. I heard Haru-san talking about him today at the market. He is going to . . ."

Father held up his hand to stop her from talking. "Okei-chan, I am sending you to America with Herr Schnell."

"But . . . but, Father! Why? Why would you send me there?"

Her father answered with gentleness. "I am sending you away from the war – and Herr Schnell needs a nanny and a seamstress."

Okei was stunned. "Please, Father, do not send me away! I do not want to go to America!"

"There is nothing for you to say, Okei-chan. Schnell-okusan is known to be a kind lady. Their nanny is too old to travel to America, and Matsu has suggested that you go in her place. The old one will teach you how to be a nanny. There is no need to teach you how to be a seamstress, for your mother has trained you well."

He cleared his throat, and said quietly, "I thank Herr Schnell for taking you with them."

Okei could not believe his words. *Why is Father doing this? I will never see my family again. I do not want to go, even if fighting does come to Wakamatsu.*

Okei looked to Mother for help. "Please, Mother, say something! Stop Father from sending me away!" Mother did not speak.

In her heart, Okei pleaded with Father but said nothing more, for she was taught to always obey him.

Father was not finished talking. "Okei-chan, tomorrow the sun will no longer shine on our house. When you leave you will take your laughter and your songs with you, but in America you will be free from war, from the turmoil that has come to Japan."

"Mother and I have three gifts for you, Okei-chan. First is the whistle." He picked up a small bamboo whistle and put it in her palm. "Over the years I have made many of these for you. If you find life to be difficult, hold it and remember family. If you lose it, it does not matter, for it is of no value in itself."

Father held out a bright red paper bird. "Okei-chan, do

you remember when Mother taught you how to make *origami* birds? It will remind you of home and songs of happiness in our garden. You have always been gentle and cheerful, like the birds. If you lose the paper one, it does not matter. You can make another."

He paused for a moment and Okei was surprised to see tears in her father's eyes. Father never showed emotion.

"Third gift is something that is not easy for me to say, Okei-chan. Our love for you is our most precious gift of all, and you will never be able to lose it."

Okei bowed her head, her mind whirling with Father's words. She did not remember leaving the table, nor did she remember unfolding her *futon* (quilt-mattress) and lying on it, but she must have done both because there she was, in the middle of the night, eyes wide open, terrified of leaving everything she loved.

As she lay on her *futon*, she found herself filling her mind with memories of home and family. *Grandmother! If only Grandmother were still alive, she would argue with Father! He would listen to her!* But Grandmother was no longer here. There was nobody who could convince Father to change his mind. Nobody.

Father, she cried silently, *Please do not send me away. Please, Father, I am not afraid of the war! I am only afraid I will never see you again.*

Sleep did not come easily to Okei that night.

— Chapter Three —

Okei Leaves Home, September 1868

Okei awoke the next morning to the cheerful sound of a bird singing in her father's garden. "Cheep-cheep-cheep! Cheeaa! Cheeaa!"

She covered her ears. *I do not want to hear a happy bird this morning. Doesn't that silly bird know I will never be happy again?*

All morning Mother and Okei talked to each other and cried together. They gathered Okei's small belongings and placed them on a *furoshiki* (large square cloth). She would take a light quilt Grandmother had made, a warm padded jacket, two *yukata* (cotton *kimono*-like dresses), *tabi* (socks), underclothes, a comb, and a few personal items. Mother added the red silk *kimono* (Japanese silk dress) that had been her mother's and her mother's before that and even farther back than that.

Okei looked at Mother's hands holding the *kimono* and she did not see trembling, she saw only gentleness and love – and she was not able to reach forward to take anything from her mother's hands. She could only watch, her face wet with tears, as Mother finished putting everything on the *furoshiki* and tied the four corners together. Mother took out another *furoshiki* for Okei's *futon*. It did not take very long to pack her meager belongings.

11

Matsu, the samurai, arrived early in the afternoon to take Okei to the Schnell house. Okei had been ready for hours. She was wearing her indigo blue *yukata*, soft from many washings yet not showing age. Her hair was neatly pulled back at her neck and secured with a colorful silk bow. Matsu greeted Okei's parents, then picked up the heavier bundle and slung it across his back. Mother helped her daughter put the lighter bundle on her back.

Okei bowed low to Father and Mother, her heart burning with sadness. She looked at Father pleadingly, wanting him to let her stay, but he said nothing. Tears streamed down Mother's cheeks. Finally Okei turned and followed Matsu as he led her away from home.

They walked a long distance, toward the other side of town, and sometimes the unwanted tears came and she could not stop them. Her mind was numb. She put one foot in front of the other and moved forward, following Matsu.

More than an hour passed before they stopped to rest. Matsu sighed as he placed his bundle on the ground and turned to Okei. He spoke to her with compassion in his voice. "Okei, I know you are not afraid of the war, but your father expects battles to come here, to Wakamatsu, and if that happens, his worst fear is that you might be killed. He is giving you a chance for a new life, a happy life, in America."

"Matsu-san, I do not want to go." She brushed her sleeve across her face, wiped the tears away, took a deep breath, and asked hesitantly, "Are there other Japanese people in America?"

"Only a few, Okei, and not where we are going. We are going to a small town in California. It is called Gold Hill." He smiled. "Schnell-san says there are beautiful hills there, not so different from what you see in Wakamatsu. The land is good for farming and people are friendly. They are hard-working people, just like us, and some of the neighbors are from Schnell-san's home country. When this war is over, he thinks more people from Japan will go to America."

He looked toward the castle. Then he spoke again. "If Lord Matsudaira survives, there will be a safe haven already established in America for him to go to – the Wakamatsu Tea and Silk Farm Colony." Matsu picked up the bundle. "Come, Okei, let us continue our journey."

They had only gone a short distance when Matsu stopped again and explained further. "Okei, I promised your father that I would protect you. I am your brother's friend and I am a samurai. I will always honor that promise."

They walked for another hour, finally reaching Herr Schnell's house. Matsu opened the gate. They followed a stone path to the front of the house and climbed the few steps where Mrs. Schnell greeted them at the door.

"Konnichiwa" (good afternoon). "Please come in, Okei. We are happy that you will be joining us."

Okei, feeling shy, forced herself to look at Mrs. Schnell and was relieved to see kindness in her eyes. She bowed low, and showing no signs of sadness, responded clearly, *"Konnichiwa,* Schnell-okusan."

Okei slipped out of her *geta* and stepped up into the house. She took her bundles and followed Mrs. Schnell to the room she would share with Frances and the old nanny. It was a pleasant room, bright with sunlight coming through an open *shoji* (sliding door), empty except for *futon* folded neatly on shelves. She put her bundles on the *tatami* (straw mat) covered floor and again followed Mrs. Schnell.

They stopped in the entryway to put on their *geta* and went along the path to a garden at the back of the house.

Okei had not noticed the garden when she first arrived. Lush green moss spread out from the house, leading to a pond and the Tearoom. Water flowed down a creek and into the pond, bubbling over a cluster of rocks and continuing on its journey toward the sea, far, far away. *Koi* (fish) swam lazily in the water. At the edge of the pond, near the Tearoom, a stone frog with baby frogs on its back kept watch over all.

Flowers grew everywhere, bursting with bright autumn colors, bringing joy into the garden. *How pretty,* thought Okei as she listened to birds singing. The loneliness of leaving home was softened by their cheerful music.

Suddenly Mrs. Schnell laughed and kneeled down. She reached forward and caught the little girl who was running toward her, then motioned for Okei to kneel beside her on the moss.

"This is Frances-chan, my daughter," said Mrs. Schnell as she tickled the toddler and made her giggle. "And this will be your new nanny, Frances-chan. Will you say hello to Okei, please?"

Okei smiled at the little girl who was now standing in front of her, struggling to say the words of greeting, so small yet already showing her mother's beauty.

"*Konnichiwa,* Okei," she said softly, then bounced back into her mother's arms.

"*Konnichiwa,* Frances-chan," said Okei, feeling not so sad now.

She looked up and saw an old woman in a dark blue *yukata* walking slowly toward them, leaning lightly on a cane.

This must be the nanny, thought Okei as she stood and bowed graciously. *She must be very old! My own grandmother did not have as many wrinkles as this nanny.*

Mrs. Schnell introduced the two women to each other, then excused herself and led Frances away.

Okei waited patiently, expecting to learn her duties.

"You are very young," said the old nanny, though not unkindly, as she peered at Okei with a questioning look in her eyes. "You look strong enough. Do you like children?"

"Yes, I do," responded Okei, answering honestly.

"What can you teach a child, then?" the nanny asked as she walked unsteadily back and forth, keeping her eyes focused on Okei.

I think this nanny is very wise, thought Okei. Wanting to be respectful, she replied politely, "I do not know. I have never been a nanny before, but I am a good seamstress."

The old nanny stopped pacing and nodded, as though pleased with the answer. "So, half the job is already done, and now I shall teach you the other half."

Chapter Four

Leaving Wakamatsu, Late September 1868

Okei was basically a happy person and instinctively liked other people. She had worked with her mother in the garden all her life. She had learned how to feed, water, train, and nurture the plants. She could even sing with the birds! She tackled the nanny job with the same vigor and cheerfulness and soon found it to be a pleasant task.

Okei was expected to be with Frances all the time unless the girl was sleeping or spending time with her parents. Then she could do laundry and sewing as needed. Before the week was over, Okei had sufficiently learned her duties. The old nanny retired to her son's home nearby, and Okei was now the nanny for Frances.

Herr Schnell traveled constantly, searching for expert silk growers and gardeners, collecting plants, silkworms, and supplies. In a short time, the household consisted of only Mrs. Schnell, Frances, Matsu, and Okei. The four became comfortable companions.

Okei's contact with her own family was minimal. Sometimes one of her brothers would bring fresh produce to the Schnell house and Okei would find a note or small drawing from her mother in the basket. She treasured these small mementos.

Toward the end of the month Herr Schnell returned home to spend time with his wife and daughter. He told of battles waging and fierce fighting far away, yet Okei sensed this could change soon. Herr Schnell said it would only be a matter of days before they must all leave Wakamatsu.

On his last day with the family, Herr Schnell led Okei into the garden, away from the ears of his young daughter. He spoke to her clearly and without hesitation. "Okei, you are my daughter's nanny and as such I expect you to protect her against all harm. Do you promise to do that?"

Okei was so nervous she wondered if she was visibly shaking. She was surprised that he had led her aside to talk to her, for after all, she was only the nanny and she did understand that her job was to take care of Frances. She nodded her head. "Yes, Schnell-san."

He continued. "I want you to understand the danger that will confront you so that you can be prepared. The Chosu and Satsuma soldiers have pillaged and burned entire towns. They have taken over most of the Tokugawa castles. They are vicious in their attacks and are killing all those who oppose them. Ours is the last Tokugawa stronghold. If we lose this battle, the new emperor will not look kindly on those who supported the Tokugawa rulers. If we lose this battle, our only hope for survival is to leave the country."

He stopped short, placed his hand on his sword handle, gripped it tightly, and then continued. "Okei, I am not saying I will desert Lord Matsudaira, but I will be prepared to save my family if our castle falls to the enemy. Tokugawa samurai are honorable and fearless, but these so-called imperial soldiers are like oozing mud, willing to smother and destroy everything in their way, even their fellow countrymen."

He looked toward the far end of the garden where Jou and Frances were laughing together, then turned back to Okei, a smile appearing and disappearing quickly. He continued his instructions.

"Your journey away from here will be difficult. We are not the only people who are fleeing Wakamatsu, but for my family it will be more dangerous. It is well known that I supplied weapons to Lord Matsudaira and pledged my support to him."

He glanced quickly at his wife and daughter again, but this time there was no smile as he gave Okei her final instructions. "You will travel to my brother's warehouse in Niigata. If you are stopped by enemy forces and questioned, you must not tell them who my wife and daughter are. You must never forget that their lives and yours depend on what I am telling you. Matsu will guide you and he will protect all of you. Above all else, you must keep Frances-chan safe."

By the time Okei woke up the next morning, Herr Schnell was gone. Soon the rest of the household would leave, also. They waited until it was dark, then left quietly. They took only what was necessary for the journey to Niigata and only what they could carry – *futon,* clothes, and food. Matsu wore his swords. The longer one, the *katana,* he placed in its scabbard at his waist and the shorter one, the *wakizashi,* next to it. He could reach either one easily.

They traveled for several days, heading west to the coast. They slept outside, hiding, wherever they could find shelter. There were checkpoints between villages, but Matsu had often traveled these roads and he was able to lead his small group around them. They skirted the checkpoints because they did not want to be questioned. It was not customary to talk to strangers, so they did not have to talk to other travelers. They feared only the soldiers.

Within the week, they were at the warehouse in Niigata. From there, they took a ship around Honshu to Yokohama. In Yokohama other members of the tea and silk colony were gathered together in a second warehouse owned by Herr Schnell's brother, Edward. There was much relief when John Henry Schnell's family arrived.

Herr Schnell was still traveling back and forth from Yokohama to Wakamatsu. He found a carpenter who was willing to go to America. He arranged for a doctor and his wife to be part of the group. He gathered tea plants, silk worms, mulberry trees, and other supplies and stored them in the warehouse until it was time to ship them to America.

As soon as his family arrived in Yokohama, Herr Schnell returned to Wakamatsu to meet with Lord Matsudaira one last time. Matsu traveled with him. They rode off on horseback and Okei was sure they intended to join forces with the samurai in Aizu. She had overheard Herr Schnell's conversation with Matsu. The imperial soldiers were now at the outskirts of town, and the battles were not going well for the Aizu samurai. She feared for the safety of her family.

Herr Schnell was gone for a month. He returned to Yokohama early in November and immediately called everyone together. The news he shared was not good. Usually his voice was loud and forceful, but as soon as he started talking to the workers and gardeners standing in the warehouse, his voice wavered.

"The people of Wakamatsu including most of our samurai are inside the castle," he said. "The imperial soldiers have destroyed the town and have pillaged even farther into the whole countryside of Aizu."

He stood before them with dented armor and torn clothes, his eyes dull, and he haltingly recounted the horror he had seen. "Those of us who remained outside fought as long as we could, but now there is nobody outside the castle, except for thousands of enemy soldiers. The Aizu samurai who were fighting outside were killed or have escaped. Some of them will come to America with us."

As Okei listened to his words, she felt the weight of silence around her and found it difficult to breathe. *What is he saying? Where are my parents? My brothers?*

She searched the faces of those nearby and found them looking just as despondent as she was. She grasped the little whistle and repeated her father's words over and over again. When life is difficult, hold it and remember family. Remember family? How could she ever forget them? If only she knew where they were and knew they were safe! She would never believe they were not alive.

She felt the grip of a small hand inside hers and looked down to see Frances staring up at her face. "Okei?" asked Frances, her little voice so soft Okei could barely hear her. Quickly she leaned down and hugged the child. "It is all right, Frances-chan," she said. "We are going to America. You and your mama and your papa and I are going to America!"

She smiled at Frances and she did not let tears fall. "See, Frances-chan? Everyone here is going to America with us, and we will go across the ocean in a very large ship. It will be a wonderful journey!"

Okei held Frances's hand as she led the child across the room to her mother. For a short moment she remembered a time when her own mother had laughed with her when she was frightened, and then she felt safe. Okei was determined to give the same comfort to Frances.

"Arigato" (thank you), "Mother," she whispered.

— *Chapter Five* —

Aboard the Pacific Mail Steamship China, May 1869

Okei stood at the ship's rail, and as she looked back toward Japan she felt a little queasy. She did not get seasick anymore, not like she did when the steamship first left Yokohama, roiling against strong winds, but when thoughts of family came to mind she still felt as if silkworms were crawling in her stomach. Even now, ten days into the voyage, it was difficult for her to believe they were halfway to America in the middle of the Pacific Ocean.

Father had been right. Fighting did come to Wakamatsu. The Aizu samurai fought gallantly and kept the Chosu/Satsuma soldiers at bay for a month until they were finally heavily outnumbered. More than five thousand people took refuge in the castle, nearly three thousand of them being samurai. When the imperial forces stormed the castle on the Fifth of November, they killed at least two thousand people. Lord Matsudaira surrendered and was escorted away, his fate unknown. As the enemy forces left the castle, they set fire to the town. The dark, bulging smoke clouds could be seen from miles away. Survivors fled to other parts of Japan. The war was over, the town of Wakamatsu destroyed, and a very young Meiji, younger even than Okei, was declared emperor of Japan.

Now, six months later, Okei was on a steamship headed to America. Okei sighed and tried to put thoughts of home and family behind her as she turned to look at the small group clustered next to her on the foredeck.

Herr Schnell was leaning against the rail, a smile on his handsome face as he watched his wife and daughter, each wearing a bright *kimono*, enjoying a happy moment together. Okei could see pride in his pale blue eyes as he looked at his small family. His wife Jou was so lovely that people often smiled when they looked at her. Her silky black hair was pulled back in the traditional Japanese knot and secured with a jeweled comb. Jou reached down to smooth her daughter's short, bobbed hair. Except for the short hair, Frances was a miniature of her mother, but when she smiled she was her father's daughter. Okei saw Herr Schnell catch Frances's attention. He worried his upper lip until his magnificent mustache quivered, causing his daughter to laugh. Her laughter rippled joyously in the salty air.

The happy sounds brought sharp memories of her own father, and she was caught in a moment of remorse. As the distance from Japan increased, so did her sense of loss. She remembered how her father's eyes would always light up when she danced. She wanted to share laughter with him, and most of all she wanted to hear him call her "Okei-chan" again. She swallowed the large lump in her throat that was threatening to explode and instead forced herself to be calm.

The weather was warm today with intermittent winds. The ocean appeared to be no different than it had been for the last ten days. Water and sky – that was the view every day, except during sunrise and sunset, and then the sun would amaze them! It would send out a wide array of red and gold colors that would splay out across the horizon. Okei and Frances watched the beautiful display every night.

The *China* was a large steamship, a side-wheeler, with huge paddle-wheels on each side that turned continuously. It was not an uncomfortable vessel. The top deck, the Spar Deck, had a walking path that ran the entire length of the

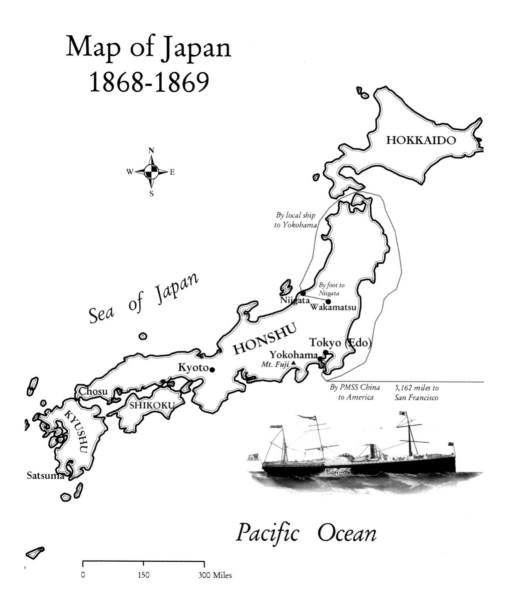

Map of Japan
1868-1869

N
W E
S

HOKKAIDO

By local ship
to Yokohama

Sea of Japan

By foot to
Niigata

Niigata

Wakamatsu

HONSHU

Tokyo (Edo)

Kyoto

Yokohama

Mt. Fuji ▲

By PMSS China   *5,162 miles to*
to America   *San Francisco*

Chosu

SHIKOKU

KYUSHU

Satsuma

Pacific Ocean

0   150   300 Miles

ship. No matter if the weather was warm or cold, passengers were on that deck. Okei felt as though she had already walked from Yokohama to San Francisco twice! She loved the feel of the wind on her face and the friendliness of other passengers.

Frances was not lacking for playmates. There was another family in a nearby cabin with several children. Frances and her doll, each dressed in *kimono*, shared many tea parties with these children.

Meals were held in the dining saloon on their deck, the Main Deck. During meals Herr Schnell talked about the ship and how it ran on coal that made steam to keep the paddlewheels churning. The ship was one of four wooden hulled ships built by the Pacific Mail Steamship Company to carry mail from China to Japan to America and back again on a regular schedule. The *China* was fairly new, less than three years old, and she was kept spotlessly clean. There were sails on the ships but they were kept furled for these trips.

Herr Schnell spent a great deal of time with other gentlemen in the Smoking Room on the Spar Deck. As soon as the ship's captain sent out the announcement –"Smoking lamp is lit!" – Herr Schnell would go to the large room to smoke his pipe and visit with other gentlemen passengers and the captain. Smoking was not allowed anywhere else because threat of fire was extremely high, especially when lamp fuel or cooking fuel was being carried around the ship.

The *China* had left Yokohama on the First of May. Okei had followed Herr Schnell and his family up the gangplank and into the large social hall on the Spar Deck where passengers received their cabin assignments. The Schnell family and Okei were in the First Class section, one deck below, on the Main Deck. There were thirty cabins on the Main Deck, fifteen cabins on each side of the aft end with the dining saloon running down the middle. Others from the Wakamatsu colony group were assigned to cabins on this deck or on the Steerage Deck, one deck below. The forward section of the Steerage Deck was for steerage passengers. Herr Schnell said there were more than a thousand Chinese in steerage and many people from other countries, too. The Chinese, by preference, had their own galley with their food prepared by a Chinese cook.

When the passengers arrived on board they were told that on the Eleventh of May they would meet the *Japan*, a sister ship of the *China*, at the midway point as she headed back to Japan from San Francisco. During most of the voyage it appeared to Okei that theirs was the only ship on this vast ocean, so it was with great anticipation that she waited for the meeting of the two ships.

Hooee! Hooee! That was the sound of the ship's whistle, the signal to proceed outside, on deck, for the captain's speech. Okei took Frances's hand and followed the Schnells out of the cabin, stepping over the raised door base, and then outside through the heavy door. Passengers were already lined up next to the rail. As she looked over the side, she could see people at the rails on all three decks. Excitement was contagious, everyone laughing and talking together.

The captain walked up and down the deck, stopping often to talk to passengers. Okei thought the captain looked quite cheerful, as though he was offering them a great surprise. His eyes seemed to sparkle as he said, "Soon you will see our sister ship, the *Japan*, appear on the horizon. She will look like our ship, with one black smoke stack." Then he walked on, talking to other passengers.

Okei looked and searched steadfastly for the steamship.

Herr Schnell had brought a telescope, and Okei was delighted when it was her turn to use it even though she saw nothing but sky and water. Herr Schnell was the first to notice a speck of black on the horizon. Okei heard the cheers as others saw the speck too. She watched it grow steadily larger until finally she could see the distinctive black hull, one black stack, and the white trim of the Pacific Mail's Steamer *Japan*. Soon the ships were stopped in the water, side by side, facing opposite directions.

The captain had told them the *Japan* would send a gig to the eastbound vessel. It was always westbound to eastbound. The ships would exchange mail and news. Some of the *China* passengers had written letters to send back to Yokohama. Okei had not. She felt pangs of sadness as she saw the large leather pouch, strapped and buckled, filled with letters, ready to be transferred to the other ship. Included in the packet was a letter from Herr Schnell, probably to his brother Edward.

Okei watched, spellbound, as a gig, carrying a group of sailors and swaying slightly, was extended out from the *Japan* on a huge wooden beam and lowered into the water, oars at the ready. As soon as the small boat landed in the water the crew rowed steadily toward the *China*.

Without warning, the wind whipped through the space between the two ships and the gig tilted. Okei watched in horror, not believing the boat would stay afloat. It tipped up and down dangerously in the violent waves and it seemed like an eternity before the wind receded. The crew, maintaining their hold on the long oars, managed to keep the gig afloat and finally reached the *China*. The sailor with the mail pouch reached for the ladder on the side of the ship and pulled himself up. He gave a sharp salute to the captain, turned over the mail pouch, and received the one for Yokohama. The crew remained steadfast as the sailor descended the ladder and climbed back into the gig. Amidst cheers and waves the small boat returned to the *Japan*.

Okei had been shocked at the near accident, and now she turned to look at the captain to see his reaction. The captain did not seem bothered at all. Instead, he looked quite proud. His hands were still clasped behind his back and he seemed to be very much at ease. He winked at Okei and said, "We have never lost a man during the mail transfer and we never will." Herr Schnell translated the captain's words.

Okei watched with relief and excitement as the gig was safely raised back onto the *Japan*. "Hoorah! Hoorah!" called out the passengers on the ships. Ladies took the scarves off their heads and waved them grandly. Hooee! Hooee! The horns of both ships joined in celebration; the walking beams of the ships bowed to each other; gunshots were heard from each deck; the meeting of the ships was ended. With great groaning the paddle-wheels churned, the ships slowly picked up speed, and then headed away from each other – the *China* to San Francisco and the *Japan* to Yokohama.

The captain looked at his pocket watch and nodded. He appeared to be pleased. He walked along the deck, nodding and talking to passengers, as the *China* continued on her journey.

Herr Schnell turned away from the departing steamship and looked at the small group surrounding him. He laughed, his enthusiasm seemingly buoyed by the meeting of the ships. "That was exciting!" he announced. "And now we are halfway to America!"

He took the silk scarf from around his neck and held it out so it flew like a flag. "We are going to make silk as fine as this in America. Someday the Wakamatsu Tea and Silk Farm

Colony will be known all over the world!"

Smiling, Mrs. Schnell said to her husband, "Your dream is good, John-san. My father was right. You have the courage of a samurai and the heart of an adventurer. It would give him great pleasure to see you now."

Okei glanced at Matsu, who was standing next to Herr Schnell. Matsu never raised his voice. He was not as tall as Herr Schnell, but he stood so straight that he looked tall. His eyes could be as piercing as a sword. He always looked balanced and ready to move quickly if necessary. Right now those piercing ebony eyes turned toward Okei as though he sensed her eyes upon him, and they sparkled as he looked at her.

I wonder if he will always see me as a little girl, she thought, *always bothering him when he was with my brother.* She had not been a child for a long time. She was seventeen years old now! She had already traveled hundreds of miles, by foot and by ship, and even though she had not fought, she had survived a war.

Okei looked away from Matsu so he could not see into her eyes. Outwardly she was composed and pleasant, a proper Japanese nanny. Inwardly, in spite of her brave thoughts, she was sad and lonely. Watching the Schnell family reminded her of what she would never have again – her own family together, her mother smoothing her hair, her father making her laugh. It would embarrass her if Matsu could see her pain. She wanted him to see only her strength.

Okei looked instead at the couple standing next to Matsu, the highly respected doctor and his wife. *Takano-okusan is tall for a Japanese lady, and she is different in other ways, too,* she thought. *She does not walk behind Takano-san like most wives do. She walks beside him, and they talk together. She is a kind lady.*

The doctor's wife smiled at her, and Okei smiled shyly in return.

Okei brought her eyes back to Herr Schnell and thought of the importance of his mission. She, Okei Ito, was part of this special group, and yes, they would start a new colony in America, and they would even name it after their hometown Wakamatsu. As the ships drew farther and farther apart she pulled her mind away from the ship that was going to Japan and focused instead on the one that promised to lead her to a happy future.

She felt a strong stirring of adventure as she faced the wind and whispered, "*Sayonara*, Father. I am going to America!"

—Chapter Six—

Arriving in San Francisco, May 20/21, 1869

O**kei** was very excited when the *China* docked in San Francisco. She stared at the scene playing out on the dock, not wanting to miss anything. Yokohama had been a busy city, but San Francisco seemed to have more confusion, more noise. She saw no other Japanese, but she did see Chinese men, just like the ones on the ship, each with a long braid hanging down his back. She thought of Matsu, who no longer wore his hair in a samurai queue at the back of his head. Many samurai cut off their queues when Meiji became emperor of Japan. Matsu waited until he was on board the ship. For seven hundred years the queue and the sword were outward signs of being samurai. Okei knew that now the honor of being samurai would reside only within Matsu's soul.

Okei's attention was caught by continuous motion around her. Ladies with their long skirts and tightly fitted jackets walked sprightly along the boardwalks, heads held high, their fancy hats sprouting tall bright feathers. Most of the men sported mustaches or beards, and wore wide brimmed hats that curled up around the edges. There were mules, wagons, horse-pulled carts, dogs, and dust everywhere. What she did not notice was that many people were staring at the Schnell group, too.

Okei held Frances's hand as they walked along the dock while Frances held on to her doll tightly with her other hand. They followed Herr Schnell, weaving their way through vendors and travelers.

"Missy! Missy!"

Okei turned her head to see who was calling. A strange man, neither young nor old, bounced toward her. He was wearing the brightest multi-colored clothes she had ever seen. Strings of beads around his neck jingled cheerfully as he jumped up and down. He elbowed his way through the crowd and called out, "Look! Look! These will make you very pretty. Very cheap. Here, try one on."

He held out an armload of colorful necklaces.

She could not understand his words, but she knew he was a vendor. At first Okei smiled. The beads were pretty, but she did not want to buy them so she tried to go around him. He blocked her path.

"Here! Here!" he said, pushing toward Okei, almost touching her – his arm so near to her face. Then he jumped right in front of her, scaring her with his closeness. She could no longer see Herr Schnell and she panicked. She put both arms around Frances.

Suddenly the man stopped and pulled back. He turned around and approached other people, calling out, "Beads! Beads! Pretty beads!"

He did not bother her anymore.

Okei turned her head and saw Matsu standing behind her. She smiled at him. I should not have worried. I must remember that he will always protect us. He is a samurai!

Herr Schnell soon rounded up his family and friends and led them to a hotel. They would stay there for a few days, before taking a side-wheeler up the river to Sacramento.

—Chapter Seven—

By Side-Wheeler to Sacramento, Late May 1869

O**kei** heard the sound of a side-wheeler's loud whistle, and touched the whistle she wore on a ribbon around her neck. She wished Father could see the huge whistle on the steamboat and the captain strutting back and forth on the deck. The captain pulled out his pocket watch, looked at it, and smiled as the Schnell party headed toward him.

"Good!" he called out. "You're on time."

They hurried up the ramp. The *Alameda* was almost ready to leave.

"Oh!" gasped Okei as a blast of steam erupted from the tall pipe. She gripped the rail tightly, almost stumbling, as she walked up the ramp.

The captain looked down at her and said kindly, "It is only the steam. It is not going to explode. The *Alameda* is a good, strong boat."

She did not understand, but the tone of his voice calmed her and she was not really frightened. The loud noise had just surprised her. The whistle blew again and they pulled away from the dock. The large paddle-wheels on each side of the boat churned the water as they headed up the Sacramento River. It would take all night to reach Sacramento.

Okei stood on the deck, watching other boats speeding down the river to San Francisco. Another side-wheeler passed them as it steamed up the river toward Sacramento, the passengers laughing and waving. Her captain frowned as he watched it go by. Okei saw him shake his head as he spoke to Herr Schnell.

"The captain is worried," Matsu told her. "That other boat is going too fast and sometimes boilers blow up when they are pushed too hard. The passengers will be lucky if it doesn't explode."

Two hours later it was time to go to bed. Okei took Frances to their stateroom. They peered out of the porthole and saw trees, bushes, and scattered pieces of wood sticking out of the mud on the river bank. Soon the gentle rocking motion of the boat and the constant thump, thump, thump of the paddle-wheels lulled them both to sleep.

Okei awoke to the sound of gunfire. She was frightened and confused. No, she thought, please no more fighting, not here in America, too!

She heard sounds of men running, voices calling, yelling. "All hands on deck!"

Through the porthole she could see bursts of flames far ahead in the water. Explosions, not gunfire!

The captain's voice called out, "Ready the lifeboats!"

Okei felt a slight surge as the boat's speed increased. She hurriedly dressed herself and Frances. The sun was just coming up as they stepped onto the deck. Other members of the Schnell group were already at the rail. Mrs. Schnell took Frances and held her close, turning her away from the horrific scene unfolding in front of them.

The speeding side-wheeler that passed them earlier was foundering in the middle of the river. Fire poured from the boat where the boiler had exploded. Screams penetrated the sounds of explosions. Okei could see people in the water, clinging to floating debris, heads bobbing, arms waving. More explosions, more fire.

As the *Alameda* sped toward the burning side-wheeler, some of the passengers hurried forward to help, including Doctor Takano. Quickly the *Alameda* captain and the Japanese doctor set up an emergency area in the saloon. The captain was well prepared for emergencies and had a good stock of medical supplies on board.

"Drop the anchor! Lower the boats!"

Passengers and crew worked together to get small boats into the water. They pulled stranded passengers into the boats and transferred them to the *Alameda*.

Just before the injured were brought on board, Doctor

Takano looked around and spoke to Okei who was standing nearby.

"Okei," he said, "I need your help. There are many injured passengers. If you assist me, my wife will be free to work on other patients by herself. It will be difficult for you, but if you focus on what I say, not on what you see, you can be of great help."

He does not know what he asks, thought Okei. *I am not a nurse. I am just a nanny! I cannot do it.* She had never been involved in a disaster such as this. She fleetingly glanced at the people near her, hoping someone else could help the Japanese doctor, but she knew she had no choice – other than the Schnell group, nobody on board spoke Japanese. Herr Schnell and Matsu both spoke English, and they were already helping elsewhere with the rescue efforts.

"Yes, Takano-san," she said, her voice feigning calmness.

"Good! We are ready then."

Okei almost fainted when they brought the first casualties into the saloon, but she found strength by doing exactly what the doctor said. She cut clothes away from wounds and put salves and bandages on cuts. She held arms and legs steady so the doctor could work on them.

Just a few hours ago she had watched these same people waving their hats and singing cheerfully as their boat sped up the river, past the *Alameda*. She thought they might be local people, Californians, some with blond, brown, or black hair, some with light-colored skin and some with dark skin. She had not seen any Japanese or Chinese.

The doctor finished the last stitch on a deep face wound while Okei held the patient's head steady. She was not prepared for the next casualty, a young man. He must have been close to the boiler, for his burns were extensive. The clothes were seared to his body; removing them would pull away his skin. The smell of burned flesh went through her nose and stayed inside her body. The horrible smell oddly filled her soul with compassion.

His face had been spared. He did not talk but his eyes flickered wildly. He finally focused on Okei and did not turn away from her, as though he found solace in her eyes. She did not know what to do. "Takano-san," she said, "is he going to die?"

The doctor looked at the boy without flinching. "We will do our best, Okei, but that will not be enough. We will give him something for his pain. Talk to him. It does not matter that he cannot understand you."

She looked into the boy's eyes, so blue, and so wide with fear. "Please, do not die," she implored. "You are not much older than I am. You must have a mother and father who love you. Maybe you have brothers and sisters, too. The doctor is trying to help you. He is a good doctor!" Then she remembered the doctor's words; no hope for this young man. She hesitated for just a moment, but continued with renewed strength in her voice. "We will ease your pain."

She smiled at him and did not question where the courage came from. She kept talking. She talked about things and people she loved and it showed in her voice. He did not cry out, even while the doctor worked on him. Okei knew he was suffering; she could see it in his eyes. She could not imagine how he could stand it. She talked more urgently. Had it been possible she would have held his hand. Sometimes she saw hope but soon there was only pain. Even then, he did not cry out.

"You have great courage," said Okei. "I think you have the soul of a samurai." She smiled, a gentle, loving smile.

The doctor was not able to save him. When the young man stopped breathing, and the doctor pulled a sheet over his head, it was too much for Okei. That final act literally took her breath away. She sobbed gut-wrenching, heart-rending gulps. She doubled over, grasping her hands tightly together in her lap. She sobbed until the young man became her brothers and they became him. She cried for all of them. *Sayonara*, brave young man. I will never forget you.

The *Alameda* continued on its journey, carrying the passengers and crew of the damaged boat. It was a somber group that headed up the river again. *No matter,* thought Okei, *that many lives were saved, there were five who died today.*

—Chapter Eight—

Coming to Gold Hill,
Late May/Early June 1869

*I*t was late in the day when they arrived in Sacramento. Herr Schnell arranged for them to stay in a hotel that night, and hired wagons to take them to Gold Hill the following day. Okei wondered how many wagons it would take to carry hundreds of bamboo plants that were twelve feet high; five hundred vegetable wax trees, four feet high; fifty thousand three-year-old mulberry trees; numerous tea plants; millions of seeds of the tea plant; silk worms in cocoons; and

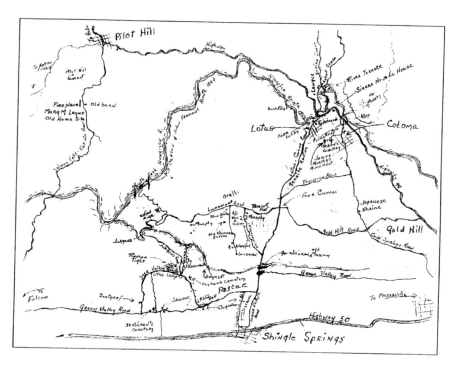

grape seedlings. Everything was packed in barrels, crates, and boxes, even their tools and personal items, including *futon*.

By noon the next day three wagons were waiting for them in front of the hotel, loaded and ready to move out, complete with drivers. Okei rode in one of the wagons with Mrs. Schnell, Frances, and Matsu. The driver kept the horses steady while Matsu lifted each of them up and into the wagon. The driver, whose name was Rusty, smiled and tipped his wide brimmed hat to each of the ladies. They nodded to him and said, *"Ohayo gozaimasu."* He responded with something that sounded like, "Howdee, Ladies." He was thin and wrinkled, but still Okei did not think he was very old, maybe not as old as Herr Schnell. His voice was deep and he appeared to be quite strong. When they were ready to go, he released the long handled wooden hand brake and snapped the reins. The horses moved forward and pulled the heavy wagon along the dirt road. Herr Schnell said it would take a day and a half to get to Gold Hill.

The roads were hard-packed, but still they were often rough and rutted. Frances bounced along, almost flying out of the wagon, laughing when it rolled over the ruts. At first, Mrs. Schnell sat up straight, as a noble Japanese lady should, even though she looked very funny trying to be very proper. In a short time, she was laughing and bouncing with Frances and Okei. The ruts soon became uncomfortable, though, and after a while Okei was thankful when the roads were not so rough.

They passed other travelers on the road, on horseback, or in wagons. Sometimes people would smile and wave, then turn around, seemingly surprised to see Japanese travelers – including two women and a little girl dressed in bright, colorful *yukata* and wearing the straw hats they had purchased in San Francisco!

As they passed farmhouses, Okei realized the farmers were dressed quite differently from people in the large cities. The women wore funny bonnets – huge brims over the face and material hanging low over the back of the neck. Good protection from the sun, she decided, not so different from the Japanese cloth head covers. The men wore hats with wide brims. In Japan, they wore straw hats – *mugiwaraboshi* – large and round, to protect them from the sun. Men here were dressed similarly to Herr Schnell, but the women all wore long dresses, or skirts and blouses, with long sleeves. Skirts were full at the bottom, and women's shoes were black, high but-toned or laced. Men's shoes

looked so heavy Okei wondered how the men could lift their feet. Later she would learn that those shoes protected feet from the dust, dirt, and clay covering the California land.

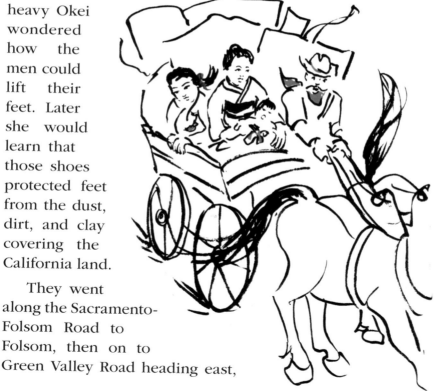

They went along the Sacramento-Folsom Road to Folsom, then on to Green Valley Road heading east, toward Gold Hill. They stopped near a creek at night. It was a pleasant evening; stars shone brightly in the sky. This was the first time they would sleep on *futon* since they left Japan. The weather was just like an early summer day in Wakamatsu, and when Okei looked up at the sky she felt a pang of homesickness. She turned her face into her *futon* and was suddenly overcome by a lingering smell of home. With one breath she was swept away, her memories so strong that she felt like a child again. She wished she were back in her mother's arms. She wished she could hear her mother's loving voice as she sang a lullaby. She burrowed into the *futon* and let tears pour out of her eyes silently. *Do you miss me, Mother? I miss you so much. Father, why did you send me away? Where are you?*

Okei knew she should not succumb to these feelings of homesickness. She willed herself to stop. She was not the only one who was sad to leave Japan. Her job was to take care of Frances and she had to put her whole heart and soul into doing that! The swirling thoughts subsided and finally she slept.

She awoke the next morning to talking and laughter, and she was determined to show the same excitement. This would be the last day of their long trip. "Look, Frances-chan," said Okei. "Look at the beautiful green hills! We will run and skip on grass as green as that and we will roll down the hills as fast as we can!" Frances giggled as she listened to her nanny. The sound brought a smile to Okei's face.

The wagon moved along slowly in its jaggedly swaying manner. Sometimes Okei looked at the mountains in the distance and was reminded of home, but she forced herself to think only good thoughts. Soon they would arrive at the Graner Farm, the place Herr Schnell had purchased for the colony. The sun was low when they reached the farm, and the sky swiftly became golden as the sun started to set, spreading a glittering blanket across the hills, a promise of good fortune to come.

The farmhouse came into full view as they rounded one of the curves. It was a large wood house, surrounded by a wide porch. The three wagons pulled up, one behind the other, in front of the house. Soon there were a few Japanese running into the yard, from inside and outside the building. As soon as they reined in the horses, the newest immigrants were surrounded and welcomed by Herr Schnell's earlier arrivals. All totaled, there were now fifteen Japanese people at the farm.

Okei thought the house was pleasing to look at. Behind it she could see many rows of healthy looking fruit trees, fully leafed, not showing yet what kind of fruit they would offer, but some of them appearing to be cherry trees. If so, the cherries should be ripe soon. On one side of the house was a creek that ran swiftly down the hill and under the road to the other side of the farm. Across the road was a vineyard.

Everywhere she looked there were trees and buildings and so much land! This farm was larger than any she had seen in Japan! Yet it had been well tended by the Graner family and seemed to be welcoming the new owners. Okei felt it was so.

The farmhouse was clean inside, the front room spacious. A big window looked out over the creek. Two other windows faced the vineyard. This room was heavy with furniture, including tapestry-covered sofas and stuffed chairs, small wood tables, short gas lamps, a large table with straight-backed chairs placed around it, and a dark, flowered rug that covered most of the floor.

In the kitchen a black stove stood on short, round legs,

and a counter on the kitchen side of the outside wall had a deep basin set into it. Okei saw another table with more chairs around it, not as fancy as the one in the front room. Directly outside the kitchen door was a huge well. A bucket hung from a thick rope ready to be lowered and raised with a pulley to draw water. Surrounding the well was a big square wall of stone, waist high, wide enough to set the bucket on without spilling the water.

There was a large bedroom on the main floor where Herr and Mrs. Schnell would sleep, and a small room behind it for Okei and Frances. Herr Schnell said they would fix up a space for Matsu on the main floor, too, at the back of the kitchen. There were beds in the big room, just like the ones in the hotels, and underneath each bed was a chamber pot. The outhouse was outside, through the door at one end of the short hall. The workers who had arrived earlier were all sleeping upstairs, as would the doctor and his wife.

Okei prepared Frances for bed and smiled at the young girl as she quickly fell asleep. Frances had been a good little traveler. Tomorrow would be soon enough to explore the rest of the house. Okei had seen stairs in the hall, but she was too tired to be curious. She could hear Herr Schnell calling to the workers as they unloaded boxes and crates, counting and checking to make sure all the supplies had arrived safely. Then she closed her eyes. That night everyone at the Wakamatsu Tea and Silk Farm Colony slept soundly.

—Chapter Nine—

Wakamatsu Tea and Silk Farm Colony, June 1869

Okei stood on the side porch looking out at the large field, already tilled and ready for planting. Soon that land would be covered with tea plants and mulberry trees as far as the eye could see. Eventually the cocoons would be placed in the middle of the mulberry trees. Until then, they would remain in the large storage area underneath the house, where it was cold and the silk worms could hibernate. The men had already planted a *keyaki* tree at the southeast corner of the farm-house. Some day it would pro-vide shade for the upstairs bedroom.

On the far side of the vine-yard, across the road, was an enormous hill with a farmhouse at the base, the home of their closest neighbors, the Veerkamps. Beyond that hill, many thousands of miles away, was Japan.

The hills surrounding the farm looked very much like those in Wakamatsu, and when Okei looked at them, she often thought of Mother and Father. She found these thoughts to be good ones, and she was not as lonely as she was when she first left home. She liked taking care of Frances and was very fond of her. Mrs. Schnell was strict, but she was also kind and even quite funny at times. Okei cared very much for this family. Suddenly she laughed out loud and said to herself, *I am a silly goose! I do not mind living in America.* Then she saw Matsu striding toward her and she thought pleasantly, *Sometimes I am very happy I am here in America!*

"*Ohayo gozaimasu*, Okei," Matsu said as he smiled at her.

Okei greeted him cheerfully, too. "*Ohayo gozaimasu*, Matsu-san." Yes, it was a good morning, and she blushed. She quickly bowed her head, hoping he could not read her thoughts.

Matsu seemed not to notice her rosy cheeks and he did not stop for very long. He was headed toward the fields. Some of the Japanese gardeners were planting mulberry trees. Others were working in the farthest section. They had already plowed the ground, tilled the soil, and dug long trenches for irrigation. Now they were placing three-year-old tea plants in mounds bordering the trenches. Water would run down the hill between the rows of plants. There should be enough rain to make the plants grow, but water in the nearby Gold Hill Ditch was available if needed. Herr Schnell had chosen to come to Gold Hill because it promised a substantial rainfall, and just two weeks earlier there had indeed been a good rain.

Herr Schnell came onto the porch with Mrs. Schnell, and looked at the men working in the fields. "It is just as I told you, Jou-san. See how beautiful this land is? These hills are just like those in Wakamatsu. If the sun continues to shine and the rain to fall, then our plants will grow strong and healthy." He looked down at her and grinned, his magnificent mustache glistening in the sunlight. "Our children will grow strong and healthy here, also." He turned, strode quickly down the steps, and headed toward the fields. There was much work to do every day now.

"If hard work brings success, then surely my husband will succeed," Mrs. Schnell said to Okei, cheerfully, as she watched her husband stride away. Suddenly, she shivered. "What is it? What brings troubled thoughts to me?" She looked around and said quietly, "The sun still shines, but it is cold, very cold!" She turned away from the sun that no longer seemed to give warmth. "Come, Okei. Let us tend to Frances. I think she is awake now."

Okei quickly followed her into the house. *Hai,* she thought. *Schnell-okusan's fear brings troubled thoughts to me, too. Is this a sign of misfortune to come?*

—Chapter Ten—

The Illness, Mid June 1869

*I**t*** was early morning and the sun had not yet shown its face. Okei was awake, listening to muffled sounds coming from the ceiling. She heard footsteps on the stairs and someone calling, "Schnell-san! Schnell-san! Come quickly. Please, hurry!"

Okei jumped out of bed, swiftly wrapped herself in her *yukata*, went to the door and opened it just a crack. Trouble, yes, but what could it be? Kuninosuke continued to knock rapidly on Herr Schnell's bedroom door.

"What is it?" asked Herr Schnell as he opened the door slightly. Now she could hear Matsu enter the hallway, too.

"Hurry, Schnell-san. The men are sick. Very sick!" Kuninosuke went back upstairs, Matsu right behind him.

Herr Schnell shut the door but soon came out fully dressed. As soon as he left his room, Okei followed, determined to find out what was happening. Her eyes quickly adjusted to the morning light. She followed Herr Schnell up the stairs and down the long hallway to the room where the workers slept. Okei stepped into the room right behind Herr Schnell and immediately reeled backward – the stench of sickness was intense!

Vomit was everywhere – on the floor, on *futon*, on the men. Most of the workers on the farm slept in this large room and they were all sick. Some were lying on *futon* shivering, moaning, and sweating profusely. Others were doubled over with pain and nausea. The room reeked of illness. Okei felt sick just looking at them.

Dr. Takano washed and dried his hands. He headed toward Herr Schnell, stepping around men and bowls of vomit.

"I have never seen anything like this," he said. "It seems as though the only ones who are sick are those who were working in the fields." He wiped his forehead with the back of his hand. *A sign of bewilderment,* thought Okei. She looked at the men and held back the taste of bile that filled her throat.

The doctor's eyes swept the room as he told them what had happened. "The men started getting sick very early this morning. At first one or two of them, and then it was as though thunder struck them all at the same time. Vomiting, pain, temperatures high. It does not appear to be food poisoning, but I do not know what the problem is."

He spoke again to Herr Schnell. "First we must try to get their fevers down. My wife will help me. I want all the workers to stay in this room. Nobody else will be allowed to come in here until we know why they are so ill."

The doctor glanced at Okei standing in the doorway, then said, "Schnell-san, I would like Okei to assist us. She was very competent on the boat."

Okei's stomach still churned with a feeling of nausea. She turned away, holding her breath, getting her emotions under control. She looked at Herr Schnell and nodded. Yes, she would help the doctor.

Herr Schnell gave his permission and returned to his family. The next day he, too, was sick with the same illness.

All planting stopped. Those who were not sick helped with the basic needs of running the farm – tending vegetable gardens, caring for animals, and preparing meals. The Japanese diet was a simple one, and the farm supplied most of their needs. Herr Schnell had brought more than a year's supply of rice to the colony. Chickens were plentiful. The men had built a pond when they first arrived, and the fish in the pond were thriving too.

The doctor, his wife, and Okei soaked cloths in herb mixtures and rubbed them on the patients' arms and legs but temperatures would not come down. The Japanese medicines did not help. Herb teas did not help. The men continued to shake with chills and drench themselves in their own sweat.

Okei washed blankets and clothes and hung them outside to dry, not wanting anyone else in the household to handle them. At times she was so tired she could think of only what she must do physically for the men – washing their room and their clothes constantly. There seemed to be no end to it. Dr. Takano and his wife were doing everything they could, but still the men were sick. None of the women became ill.

A few of the men were feeling slightly better after a few days, including Herr Schnell. The doctor looked pleased. "This is good," he said. "Now maybe the others will improve too. Our medicines must be working!"

But the medicines were not helping, and the others did not improve. The men were so weak that Okei was frightened for them. Finally, the exhausted doctor spoke to Herr Schnell. "Schnell-san, I can do nothing more. I fear some of the men will die if we do not get help." It was now more than a week later.

Herr Schnell nodded in agreement and said, "We will see if Mr. Veerkamp can help us. I will send Matsu to his farm."

Matsu took the small wagon and drove swiftly to the neighbor's farm, returning a few hours later with Mr. Veerkamp and his oldest son Henry and the local doctor.

The doctor entered the room, took a good long look at the workers, and said, "These are the men who were working in the fields, eh? Looks like your workers have a good case of what we call country fever. Those mosquitoes are nasty little devils! They've brought down stronger men than yours, but we'll cure them!"

He set his well-worn medicine bag down on the floor, opened it, and took out a large bottle of dark-colored liquid. Together, the two doctors began treating the patients.

Okei could not believe how fast the men responded! Within two days the vomiting and chills stopped. The men were able to eat again. They were able to sit up, and though still very weak, began to regain their strength. Within three weeks of the first illness, every single man was better.

Chapter Eleven

Okei's Hill,
Autumn 1869 to Early Spring 1870

*T*he first year at the farm went by quickly. In October, another group of workers arrived from Japan, thirteen of them, silk growers and farmers, some of them samurai. They came to San Francisco on the steamer *America,* then up the river to Sacramento, and by wagon to Gold Hill, just as Okei's group had done. Some of them were from the Aizu area, and Okei hoped they would bring news of her family, but there was none.

In February they received and planted 140,000 three-year-old tea plants.

In March the rain finally subsided, and Mrs. Schnell gave birth to a second daughter, Mary. Okei could not imagine that a baby would bring such joy to so many people. Mrs. Veerkamp visited frequently, especially after Mary was born. Mrs. Veerkamp had five sons and no daughters.

Mrs. Veerkamp often brought fresh bread. The smell was pungent and strong. It was sourdough bread, a funny name thought Okei, who at first also thought it had a funny taste. It tasted nothing like the flat rice cakes Mrs. Schnell and Okei made, which were quite mild in flavor.

When Mrs. Veerkamp visited, Mrs. Schnell always served tea, and today was a tea day. Both of the girls were napping. Okei set the water to boil on the stove. She placed a teapot and three Japanese tea-bowls, the size of large cups, no handles, on the table. She reached into the container of tea leaves with the tips of her fingers, grasped a small bunch of the dry leaves and dropped them into the teapot. As soon as the water came to a boil, she poured the boiling water

over the leaves, and then let the tea steep for a few minutes. Mrs. Schnell poured the tea. The aroma of fresh hot tea filled the room and enveloped the ladies in comfort as they sat in peaceful quietness.

One day after the rain had ceased, when the weather was warm and the ground dry, Okei decided to take the girls for a walk. She bound the baby to her back in a shawl with the ends securely tied around her shoulders and waist. She took Frances's hand and said, "Come, Frances-chan. Today I am going to show you my favorite place on the entire farm!"

Off they went. Okei sang cheerfully as she and Frances climbed the hill to the north of the farmhouse. She usually came here by herself when Frances and Mary were napping. Winter had been very cold and wet, the ground muddy, so Okei waited until the weather was pleasant before she brought the girls with her. Now the trees behind the house were beginning to show pink with the budding of first blossoms and she knew the hill would show signs of spring, too.

Okei carried a basket filled with fruit, rice balls, and a light quilt. She hurried up the hill just as she always did. Frances scurried along beside her. When they reached the knoll, she unfolded the quilt and spread it out on the grass underneath a tall pine tree. She very gently laid Mary, still sleeping, down on the quilt. As she kneeled back and looked around she felt happy, for the view from here reminded her of Japan.

"Look, Frances-chan," said Okei. "Look at the flowers! They are everywhere! Surely they are feeling the warmth of the sun!"

The hill today was spectacular. The wildflowers did seem satisfied that the end of winter was finally here, for they had burst forth in bunches of reds, yellows, blues, and purples.

The dirt was covered with a carpet of tender new grass, silken to the touch. Okei turned around slowly, stretching her arms out to the sun, filling herself with its warmth, while Frances imitated her. Okei began to sing as she took Frances's hands and led her in a simple Japanese folk dance. They bowed and dipped and turned, and moved their arms gracefully in and out and around. Together they danced and sang on top of Okei's hill.

Finally they bowed to each other and giggled. Okei enjoyed sharing her hill with Frances. At that moment, she felt more like an older sister than a nanny. She felt the family love an older sister would feel toward her siblings.

Okei kneeled on the quilt next to Mary who was now awake and gurgling happily. Frances scampered around the hillside, gathering wildflowers. As Okei looked out, past the hills to the west, it was easy for her to imagine herself at home, in her father's garden. She listened to a bird singing nearby, and it also reminded her of home. Okei's heart was singing, too.

"Look, Okei," said Frances as she held out a bright red feather.

Okei reached for it and smiled. "This is a bird's feather, Frances-chan. The bird is called a finch. If you are very quiet, I think you can hear him." Frances was as quiet as a four-year-old girl could be, but the bird did not appear.

Okei took a piece of rice ball out of the basket and tossed it onto the grass. Soon there was a rustling sound in the tree and a pretty red bird appeared, sitting on one of the branches. He was a funny little bird with a crossed bill. He looked at them and then at the rice ball. He tilted his head. He flicked out his tail. He fluffed up his wings. He was quite the actor for his small audience! Finally he flew down to the grass, picked up some of the treat, and then ate every bit of it. When he was finished, he flew back to the tree, fluffed himself out all over, lifted his head, and sang.

"Cheep-cheep-cheep! Cheeaa! Cheeaa!"

"Oh," said Frances. "That was pretty! More songs, please." She was delighted when the little bird bowed, as though he, too, was happy. He sang cheerfully for a long time. Too soon it was time to go back to the farmhouse.

"Will we see the little bird again?" asked Frances.

"I am certain we will," said Okei. "He is always at home when I come to visit."

As Frances skipped down the hill, Okei laughed and said, "He looks just like the birds in my father's garden."

Chapter Twelve

Trouble at the Creek, Late Spring 1870

*E*xcept for the illness shortly after they arrived, things were going rather well at the Wakamatsu Tea and Silk Farm Colony. Mary was a happy, healthy baby, and Okei was kept quite busy caring for the two girls. There was much laughter and joy in the Schnell house with its many residents. Two of the families who arrived in October had each brought a child with them, and now there were four children in the colony. Herr Schnell promised that each family would have its own small house by the following year.

When the men were working in the fields, it was difficult for Okei to tell who was Japanese and who was not. The Wakamatsu men no longer wore their traditional, short *hapi* jackets with the leggings or wrap-around pants. They now wore denim overalls or long pants, long sleeved cotton shirts, and the heavy boots that had seemed so strange when they first arrived. Now the men looked like Californians!

Herr Schnell spent many hours outside working with the men, but he also found time to play with his daughters. "He is a crazy man," laughed Mrs. Schnell. Her eyes shone as she watched her husband quietly peek at Mary, then pick Frances up and gleefully dance her around the room.

"Hai!" said Okei who was standing next to Mrs. Schnell. "Soon Frances-chan will be dancing as well as her papa!"

During the warm weather, in the evenings, they could hear

music coming from the Veerkamp Farm. Okei enjoyed listening to the sounds of the fiddle and the harmonica that floated across the fields, and the laughter that often followed. The Wakamatsu Farm had music of its own, too, for Mrs. Schnell often played the *samisen*. The Veerkamp music was fast and quick – the foot-stomping kind – whereas Mrs. Schnell's music was meant for listening. Mrs. Schnell was teaching Okei and Frances how to play the three-stringed Japanese instrument. Okei thought it was easier to pluck a chicken than to pluck the *samisen*! She smiled as she thought of many happy times here on the Wakamatsu Farm.

The tea plants continued to flourish and to grow strong. Weather was exactly what the colony needed, with plenty of rain and sun. Henry Veerkamp and Matsu had become close friends. Henry visited often, bringing gifts of bread and pies that his mother had baked. Other neighbors were friendly, also.

Because things were going well, it was unexpected one morning to find no water coming out of the Gold Hill Ditch. This was the ditch that supplied water to the farm all year long. Herr Schnell and Matsu left the house, heading toward the tool shed, then to follow the creek up the hill, to find out why there was no water.

Okei and Mrs. Schnell spent the rest of the morning cutting and sewing material. They were making a dress for Mrs. Schnell, just like the ones Mrs. Veerkamp wore, but much smaller. The dress would have a fitted bodice with buttons down the front, a full skirt, long sleeves with lace cuffs and a lace collar at the neck. They had purchased the material at Bell's store in Coloma. Okei would make one for herself, too, and she was excited at the thought of having a new dress! It would be small in size, for she was the same size as Mrs. Schnell. She would not be as beautiful as Mrs. Schnell, but she wondered if she would look pretty in the new dress.

She glanced at Frances who appeared to be happily entertaining her sister. She smiled to see that the girls were busy, too. At noon, the ladies stopped working and prepared lunch. Mrs. Schnell frequently looked out the window toward the creek.

"Okei," said Mrs. Schnell, "The men should have returned by now. I wonder if they found unexpected problems?"

Okei was worried, too. Herr Schnell and Matsu had left hours ago and the ditch was not that far away. "Shall I look for them?" asked Okei. "Surely nothing can happen to Schnell-san on his own farm! Is it the water, Schnell-okusan? Is that why you are so worried?" She was aware of arguments between farmers and gold miners over the use of water.

"Yes, Okei, I am very worried. I feel that something is wrong." Mrs. Schnell picked up the lunches that were wrapped in *furoshiki* and handed them to Okei. "All the workers are in the vineyard, so I must send you alone. Please be careful."

Okei took the lunches and headed up the hill alongside Gold Hill Ditch. She had gone quite far before she heard sounds of water trickling over rocks. Then she saw water gurgling down the creek, hesitantly at first, but soon becoming a steady flow. Good, she thought, soon I shall see Schnell-san and Matsu-san coming down the hill. But she did not encounter them, so she kept walking.

She came to the place where Herr Schnell and Matsu had pulled large branches and heavy boulders out of the creek, proof that someone had purposely stopped the water from going to the Wakamatsu Farm. She was puzzling over the pile of debris, when she began to hear voices coming from a short distance away. That was Schnell-san! She could hear him clearly. "Well, well, well," he said. "What do we have here?"

Okei continued up the hill and followed a path leading away from the creek, quietly now, trying not to make any sound, not stepping on broken branches or kicking stones. She came slowly around a bend and saw Herr Schnell and Matsu standing at the edge of a messy camp, their pants and boots dripping water. She quickly ducked down behind a bush. She could see and hear the men but knew she was well hidden.

Three grubby gold miners had been sitting around a campfire, and now one of them was standing and glaring at Herr Schnell and Matsu. Another miner started to reach for a rifle. Quickly Matsu drew his *katana* (long sword) and the man froze. He glowered at Herr Schnell.

"Watcha doin' here?" he asked angrily, tobacco spittle dripping from his mouth. "Git out of our camp! Go on, git out of here!"

"We will," said Herr Schnell calmly. "But I want to know why you would steal the water? There is enough for all of us."

"It ain't yer water!"

"Well, now!" said Herr Schnell as he took a folded paper out of his pocket and held it in front of him. "This document says it is our water."

"It makes no never mind what yer paper says," sneered the man. "It's our water!" He bunched his hands into fists, thrust his jaw forward, and spat out a shot of murky brown liquid that landed just in front of Herr Schnell's boot.

Herr Schnell did not acknowledge the man's rudeness. "This is a legal paper," he said. "It gives us the right to use the water that flows through Gold Hill Ditch. If you stop the water, you could go to jail, for we own the water rights."

He turned slightly and said, "Matsu, alert the workers.

These miners will cause more trouble if they can."

Okei crouched lower. She was frightened but she remained quiet.

Herr Schnell looked steadily at each man, then turned and strode away. He showed no fear. It was Matsu's job to ensure his safety. Okei met them as they rounded the bend. She was still carrying the lunches.

"Ah, Okei," said Matsu, "Come, there is no reason to spend more time up here with such unpleasant men. We have taken care of the problem." He took the lunches from her, said *"Arigato"* (thank you), and led her down the hill to join Herr Schnell.

Okei hoped there would be no more trouble from the men, but she had seen their faces as Herr Schnell left the camp, and she knew those men were filled with hate. She looked at Herr Schnell's face and wondered if he had eyes in the back of his head. He was leaning on his shovel, looking at the water flowing down the creek. *He knows he is not finished with the miners,* she thought. *He knows how hateful they are!*

But now her job was finished for she had given the men their lunches. She hurried back to the house to tell Mrs. Schnell about the troublesome miners. She did not think it would be wise for those men to go against Herr Schnell and Matsu. Did they know nothing about samurai?

—*Chapter Thirteen*—

Going to the Fair, June 1870

Okei was caught up in the excitement at the farm. Today Herr Schnell would take his teas to the San Francisco Horticultural Fair. The mulberry trees were thriving, providing food for the silk worms, and the tea plants were growing faster than expected. The Wakamatsu Tea and Silk Farm Colony was doing very well indeed, and it was time to display their excellent products to the rest of the world.

Everyone on the farm was in the yard; some of the men were loading the wagon under Herr Schnell's precise directions. Okei, holding Mary, stood near Mrs. Schnell and Frances. "Look at your papa, Mary-chan," she said. "See how busy he is!"

"Watch the chests!" called out Herr Schnell. "Do not scratch them! Put the cloth between them!" The precious tea leaves were inside the chests. These were the first pickings from the three-year-old plants the gardeners had set out last year.

Kuninosuke the carpenter had made special chests of fine wood and polished them until they glowed. Herr Schnell had said to Kuninosuke, "The display boxes must be perfect so that people will expect the tea to be of the best quality, too." Carefully printed on the front of each box was "Wakamatsu Tea and Silk Farm Colony, Gold Hill, El Dorado County, California." The workers wrapped the chests in fine Japanese silk and fitted them carefully into large crates.

Herr Schnell rushed from one side of the wagon to the other. Okei thought he looked funny but she dared not smile. Back and forth he went, his coat flying out behind him as he turned around quickly, checking everything – each chest and label and oil and rope. "Where is the oil? The precious tea oil?" he yelled. "There it is, in the tall box! The tea plants? Yes, yes, everything is there. It is time to go! We must leave now!" Then he stopped, spun around, and strode toward his wife.

Mrs. Schnell handed him a *bento* box, wrapped in *furoshiki*, heavy with food. He took it from her, gave it to Kuninosuke, and said excitedly, "Jou-san, this is wonderful, is it not? The farm is successful. You see? It is true!"

He bent down, took one of her hands in both of his, and grandly brought it to his lips. He tickled Mary under the chin, whirled around once more and laughed cheerfully. "Come, Frances-chan! Come to your Papa and wish me luck!" He picked her up, spun her around, and hugged her. He put her down and strode quickly to the wagon. He and Kuninosuke settled themselves on the buckboard. He was about to flick the reins when dust began to rise up along the road.

Two wagons were rapidly arriving, one behind the other. "Whoa!" called out Mr. Veerkamp from the first wagon as he pulled on his horses' reins. Mrs. Veerkamp was sitting beside him and their five sons were hanging over the sides in the back, yelling boisterously and waving their hats. Mr. Veerkamp called out, "Glad we caught you, John. Louisa didn't want you to head out without taking one of her pies with you." Mrs. Veerkamp smiled as she passed the pie over. It was wrapped in a bright red and white cloth.

The second wagon pulled up, driven by another neighbor. "Herr Schnell," he said, "your teas are the best I have ever tasted. Good luck at the horticultural fair!" He handed over a package that smelled deliciously like freshly baked bread.

"Thank you," said Herr Schnell to each of them. Then he said quite loudly, "Does everyone in California know I am taking my teas to San Francisco? How wonderful!" He sat up very straight, twirled his magnificent mustache, and smiled broadly. He flicked the reins, and the horses pulled the wagon away from the farm. Okei smiled. She thought Herr Schnell looked very happy today!

—Chapter Fourteen—

Shopping in Coloma, July 1870

Okei sat in the wagon outside Bell's Store in Coloma, waiting for Matsu to finish loading their supplies. She looked at the remains of Sutter's Mill where logs were milled and where the first gold nugget was found in 1848. She had seen gold nuggets. Herr Schnell kept a few of the yellow pebbles in his pocket, and sometimes pulled them out so his family, including Okei, could look at them and hold them. She was amazed that something so small could have been so valuable.

She heard that people had come from all over the world just to search for gold in California. Coloma was a busy town from 1848 to 1854. At first the miners found lots of gold but then there were too many people and the gold was harder to find. Most of the businesses eventually closed down and people moved on. Now there were very few miners, and they usually kept to themselves. Sometimes, though, they would come into town for a bath or a hotel meal.

Okei gazed at the material she had just purchased, a pretty blue calico. She ran her fingers over it, enjoying the feel of new cotton, soft and smooth. *Now I can make another dress for Frances-chan, who is growing fast and is tall for a four-year-old. I will make a dress for her just like the ones the neighbor girls wear, with buttons down the front and a full gathered skirt. I will make one for Mary-chan, too.*

She smiled as she thought about the hat Herr Schnell

brought back from San Francisco for Frances. It was much too fancy for the country, but Frances loved it and wore it every day. It was blue, the same shade as the calico material, and prettied up with ribbons and lace.

Herr Schnell returned with good news from the San Francisco Horticultural Fair. The colony's products received great reviews in the newspapers and there would be no problem finding buyers for all the tea and oil they could produce.

The wagon shifted slightly as Matsu put a large bag of flour into the back. Okei came quickly out of her thoughts. As she turned around, she saw three men swaggering up behind Matsu. They stopped only a few feet away from him.

"Hey! Lookey, there!" said one of the men, pointing his bony finger at Matsu.

Okei recognized them as the unpleasant miners, the scruffy men who had stopped the water from coming down their creek. The most obnoxious one, the miner they referred to as Lockjaw, said, "There's those durned foreigners who'r steal'n our water!"

He spat into the dirt just inches away from Matsu's boot. Okei froze. She turned white with fear. She did not understand what he said, but she felt the hatred. The miners' mouths twisted into ugly snarls, their eyes became malicious stares. Matsu ignored them, climbed into the wagon, and snapped the reins. The horse pulled the wagon neatly away, and soon they were headed out of town.

"Okei," said Matsu, "that is an evil man. He is selfish and greedy. Do not ever let him see fear in your eyes. Be strong."

She looked at Matsu and said quietly, "Did you see him look at us, Matsu-san? He is filled with hate."

"He hates us because we have the water. He wants the

72

water to help him flush out the gold, but the water is not his." Matsu paused, as though thinking, and then he continued. "I do not trust those men. They know Schnell-san has legal rights to use the water. They want all of it for themselves. You must always be watchful, for they will harm us if they can."

Both of them were quiet the rest of the way home. As the wagon rolled along, Okei tried to imagine what the miners might do. *Are those men really as dangerous as Matsu-san says? Is it gold that causes such hatred?* She gripped the side rail tightly as she thought about the girls and recalled the words Herr Schnell had said to her almost two years ago in the garden – "Above all else, you must keep Frances-chan safe." Now it would be both girls. *I will let no harm come to Frances-chan and Mary-chan! I must be ever watchful.*

Okei's commitment to protect the girls quickly overcame her fear.

—Chapter Fifteen—

Trouble in the Fields, Late Summer 1870

*L*ate one night Okei was awakened by strange noises. She listened to the night sounds and did not like what she heard. Someone was in one of the fields, and she sensed there was trouble.

She heard Matsu leave the house, so she dressed quickly and followed him. He was moving fast toward the sounds of laughter, eerie laughter. The moon was full, giving light, and Okei followed him easily up the hill behind the house. When they reached the end of the mulberry trees, where a row of bushes separated the trees from the tea plants, he stopped so fast that she almost bumped into him. She came up beside him, peered through the bushes and saw . . . nothing. The beautiful tea plants were gone!

Her heart raced. This was not possible! The entire field of tea plants had disappeared. Her head swiveled back and forth, eyes searching, seeking. Then she realized the plants were not gone, they had been smashed! She felt the burning heat of rage. Yesterday there were rows of healthy looking tea plants in this field. Now there was just a mess of trampled leaves and branches.

Laughter again. Where was it coming from? She knew the reason for the laughter now, but who was doing it? The only person she could see was Matsu. He had made no sound. Was he made of steel, like the blade of his sword? Before she could say anything, he motioned for her to remain quiet. They stayed crouched down, behind the bushes, not moving.

Okei heard voices coming closer.

Three men walked right past them. Okei recognized them as the miners and she quickly stopped herself from making any sound.

"That was a good job!" said one of the miners.

"Yeah," said another. "That's a right fine mess!"

They laughed and then kicked out at the trodden plants. Two of them walked away, but the third man, Lockjaw, stayed behind, gloating over the damage.

Matsu slowly drew his *wakizashi* (short sword) and quietly came up behind the miner. He reached around and pressed the sharp edge of the sword firmly against the man's throat. Okei saw the quiver of fear that flowed through Lockjaw as Matsu spoke into his ear. "You are an evil man and you have harmed us twice, but you will not do it again. If you hurt us again, you will be gone. Do you know what I mean by gone?" He waited until Lockjaw nodded. "Do not think your friends can hurt us either. This whole town would like to be rid of all three of you!"

Matsu slowly released his hold on the miner and watched him stumble toward the creek. "May this be the end of our problems with you," he said. His steel black eyes followed the direction Lockjaw had taken. *"Sayonara,* Lockjaw!"

Matsu sheathed his sword and looked at the broken plants. He stood there, not speaking for a moment. Then he bent down and picked up a few of the damaged leaves. He clenched his jaw and spoke slowly. "The workers will have to clean up this field and replant anything that can be salvaged. Tomorrow's sun will not bring happiness to Schnell-san and the workers."

Matsu threw the broken leaves away and turned back to

Okei. She was sure she saw anger in his face, but his words said otherwise. "Okei, we cannot allow *haraga tatsu* (deep anger) to fill our minds. We must follow forward thoughts, not backward anger."

She knew those were samurai words! She looked at him. Not be angry? There was meanness behind the act and she was furious! She said nothing. Why should she not be angry? They had all worked hard to make this farm a success!

She followed Matsu back to the house, stomping steadily along, each firm step reminding her of the trodden plants. She thought of the gardeners and how horror stricken they would be when they saw the field the next day, and then she began to feel sad. Still, she was not samurai, and it would not be easy for her to replace anger with good thoughts. She gritted her teeth, let out a deep breath, and said hopefully, "*Sayonara,* Lockjaw."

Chapter Sixteen

The Drought,
February 1871

Matsu was worried. Okei could tell by the way he looked at the sky that it was so. She was hanging clothes out to dry while Matsu and Henry stared at the clouds, watching them sail by – dry clouds, not ones that could give them rain.

Matsu picked up a handful of dirt and let the dry, dusty soil fall between his fingers. Then he looked at the sky again.

"Those aren't rain clouds, Matsu," said Henry. "They're just 'teasers' letting us get some hope in our minds. Nope, those aren't going to help at all." He sighed deeply. "Besides, I haven't heard the frogs croaking, and my father says that's a sure sign there isn't going to be any rain soon."

The two men had become good friends, even though Henry was Okei's age and Matsu was ten years older. The men leaned on the fence and watched the Japanese workers carry buckets of water from Gold Hill Ditch, trying to save as many plants as possible. The water in the ditch was low, but still flowing.

All the farmers were conserving water, letting some of their crops die and trying to save what they could. At least the gold miners weren't bothering them anymore! Okei shivered as she remembered the trampled plants and the stunned looks on the workers' faces the following morning. That was six months ago and now they had a different problem – a dry winter.

Matsu spoke slowly. Okei could understand English much better now. "Henry, if we do not have rain soon, I do not think the colony will survive. See how small our plants are? The only thing growing strong is the *keyaki* tree, but only because it is near the farmhouse." He smiled at Henry. "Even your mother waters that tree when she comes over. One day that tree will be so big your children will be swinging under it."

"What are you talking about, Matsu? Me? Married? Children? I don't even think about girls!" His face began to turn a warm shade of crimson. Okei's face turned red at the thought of marriage, too, not with Henry of course, but . . . just marriage. Here in America, for her?

Matsu laughed, but he continued in a different manner. "Henry, the local doctor was very helpful when our workers were ill. We did not have such an illness in Wakamatsu. Our doctor, Tokano-san, did not know what to do when the fever came. Without your doctor's help, some of the men would probably have died."

Okei understood most of what Matsu was saying and she smiled. She had seen how quickly the men improved as soon as they received the medicine the local doctor brought. The doctor visited often, even bringing flowers to the ladies. He would hide the flowers behind his back, and then bring them out with a flourish and say, "Surprise!" This made them all laugh.

"Kuninosuke is making a special chest for him, to hold his instruments," said Matsu. "It is not a large gift, but we hope he will appreciate it."

"That's great, Matsu! He'll really like that. Most towns around here don't have a doctor, so I guess we're mighty lucky!" Henry grinned. "My mother makes apple pies especially for him, and he sure does enjoy them. Why, I swear, I've seen that man eat one of those pies all by himself in five minutes easy!"

Henry and Matsu fell quiet, and Okei knew they were both hoping for rain that would not fall. She too looked up at the sky and prayed for clouds to grow large and gray and bring rain.

Chapter Seventeen

Another Illness,
April 1871

As the girls played in the yard, Okei stood nearby, listening to Matsu and Henry discuss the weather. That was all anyone talked about lately. The drought had affected everything. The silkworms were dead and the plants were dying, too. Herr Schnell was preparing to go back to Japan for more plants and more money. They needed both if the farm was to survive. She did not question where the money would come from. She trusted Herr Schnell still had sources.

In spite of the troubles, Okei enjoyed watching Matsu and Henry. Matsu always stood straight and his movements were smooth and sure. Henry moved every which way. Now he had one foot on the fence rail and was sucking on a piece of straw. Ugh! He laughed a lot and was always friendly. Sometimes he laughed so hard he would take his hat off and slap it across his legs. He and Matsu laughed at each other, too. Okei did not always know what was so funny. No matter. She just enjoyed being near them.

Suddenly a pleasant thought came into her head. *Matsu-san and Henry are my best friends!* She looked at them again and smiled, then bowed her head so they would not think she was making fun of them. In Japan she would never have had two young men as her best friends!

Okei turned toward Frances and Mary. It was time for their naps, even though Frances, almost five years old, did not think she needed one anymore. Okei picked up the empty laundry basket and walked toward the girls. She had only taken a few steps when her eyes stopped focusing and her mind went numb. Her limbs were suddenly very heavy. The basket slipped from her hands as she fainted.

"Okei!" called Frances as she ran to her nanny. "Okei!" She leaned down and patted Okei's face with her tiny hands. "Wake up, Okei! Wake up!"

Hearing Frances call out, Matsu and Henry turned and rushed to Okei. Matsu kneeled down, lifted her eyelids and then felt her forehead. "Henry," he said, as he picked her up and hurried toward the house, "please bring the girls. Schnell-okusan is inside, and I think Okei has a fever." He carried Okei into the house and placed her on her bed.

Mrs. Schnell's face went pale as soon as she saw Okei. "Please get the doctor, Matsu," she said quietly. She sat beside Okei, gently wiping her face and arms with a damp cloth. Okei was breathing but she was not moving at all. Henry and the girls waited close by until Matsu returned with Doctor Takano.

Okei's body raged with a fever. She could not talk, but she could hear people talking. She felt more tired than sick – not nauseous like the men were when they first came to the farm. Her arms and legs felt so heavy, she could not move them. She knew Mrs. Schnell was caring for her, she felt the gentle hands on her body and she smelled the herbs.

Matsu did Okei's chores and he even watched the girls when they played outside. Okei could hear the children's voices, but it seemed as though they were far away. One day the sounds were especially clear.

"Sing to us, Matsu-san," begged Frances. "Okei sings to us."

"*Hai!*" he said, gruffly. "I cannot sing like a bird."

"Dance for us, Matsu-san," said Frances. "Okei dances for us."

"*Hai!*" he said. "I do not dance!"

Doctor Takano made herb dressings from lavender and eucalyptus, trying to bring Okei's temperature down. Mrs. Schnell brewed healing teas from the farm's own plants and gently forced her to drink them. Mrs. Veerkamp came many times to help in the sickroom, and sometimes she brought chicken soup for all of them. She would sit by the bed, hold Okei in her arms, and slowly feed her a spoonful at a time. She would sing to her. Okei sensed the singing and when Mrs. Veerkamp was holding her, she felt like a child again, in her own bed and in her mother's arms. She cuddled up to Mrs. Veerkamp, believing she was her mother. She was soothed. She smiled weakly.

Okei was terribly sick for many days. Finally her temperature started to come down.

One day Okei thought she was in her father's garden. She heard the birds singing and smelled the flowers. She felt happy because she saw her parents standing in the garden, talking and laughing. But why were they speaking English? She knew they could not speak English! Then she woke up and realized that she was not home; she was still in America, and there was no Mother and there was no Father.

A single tear slid down her cheek. She was more tired than she could possibly imagine and she felt so alone. As she lay there, she became aware of a pleasant fragrance. In her bedroom there were many flowers. She saw a bouquet of wildflowers and knew Frances and Mary had picked those. She heard a bird singing a cheerful song outside her window and she knew who that was!

Okei smiled wanly as she looked around her room.

"I have many friends here," she whispered. Sad thoughts of home and family were softened by these simple gifts. Slowly she continued to improve until finally she was able to go outside for longer and longer periods of time to see the beautiful hills that reminded her of Japan.

—Chapter Eighteen—

A Time of Happiness,
Early May 1871

Okei kneeled on a quilt in the yard, enjoying the warmth of the sun. She was making dresses for the girls and concentrating on keeping her stitches small and straight.

"Okei! Look, Okei!"

Okei turned, put her hands to her face, and laughed. Matsu was walking toward her, carrying two giggling little girls as though they weighed nothing at all. Matsu looked as happy as the girls, and it was easy to forget he was a samurai. Most people

would not laugh at a samurai.

Okei stood up and reached for Mary. "Thank you, Matsu-san. I still tire easily. You were kind to take the girls for a walk." She smiled at the girls and said, "And now you two little sparrows, it is time for your nap." Okei climbed slowly up the stairs as the girls bounced along beside her.

"Will you sing to us, Okei? Please? I love to hear you sing," said Frances.

"Okei," called out the samurai, smiling, "I almost forgot. We saw your little finch this morning. He was in his favorite tree and he was a happy bird today."

Okei's eyes sparkled as she stood on the porch. She smiled as she thought of Matsu kneeling on top of the hill with the girls. In spite of his strength, he was a gentle man, and she wondered if the girls had ever succeeded in making him sing and dance for them.

She was so happy that at first she did not see Herr Schnell and Mrs. Schnell standing together in the shadow of a tree. As she took the girls into the house, she happened to glance back just as Mrs. Schnell touched her husband's arm and also looked toward the house. *How odd,* thought Okei. *Schnell-okusan looks sad. What did Schnell-san say?* She felt a tremor of apprehension. Were they discussing her?

Herr Schnell turned away from his wife and headed across the road. He stopped and looked out at the fields that once were green. He watched the workers as they carried small amounts of water to the dying plants, then he slowly walked toward them.

Okei could almost follow his thoughts. "Water! All because of water." For a long time Herr Schnell had believed the colony would succeed, but lately Okei felt this was no longer so. Everyone knew he was going back to Japan to obtain more supplies and that he was taking the whole family with him. Why would Mrs. Schnell be so sad?

"Okei," said Frances, gently tugging on Okei's sleeve. She was reminded of her duties. She looked down at Frances, smiled, and herded the girls into the house. The feeling of unease stayed with her as she went inside.

—Chapter Nineteen—

Setting up for a Party, Veerkamp Farm, May 1871

Okei took a square piece of colored paper from the short stack on the picnic table. She folded and pressed, folded and pressed, then pulled on the corners and looked at the origami bird she had just made. She was sitting at a table in the Veerkamp's yard, making origami favors for the *Sayonara* Party that would be held that night. Herr Schnell would soon be leaving to go to Japan.

Matsu and Henry finished setting up tables and benches and now they were putting kerosene lanterns on the tables and hanging them on posts around the yard. There would be singing and dancing and lots of delicious food. All of the neighbors were invited. Some of the children would try to eat with chopsticks, but few had mastered the art. There would be much rice spilled tonight!

The three friends enjoyed working together. After the young men finished their jobs they joined Okei at the table. Henry picked up one of the birds, held it in the air as though making it fly, and then he turned toward his friend.

"Matsu," he said, "I can't wait to see your samurai dance tonight. You really look like a warrior when you swing that sword around."

The samurai laughed as he stood back and looked at Henry. "It is not a dance, Henry. It is more of an exercise where I show strength, discipline, balance, and patience. Those are things I apply to the way I live."

Then Matsu looked at Okei and asked, "What is the rest of it, Okei?"

She blushed and said, "Without courage, loyalty, duty, and a good heart a samurai is not a true samurai."

Matsu smiled and bowed to her, but still Henry persisted with questions. "Did you ever use your sword when you lived in Japan?"

"Yes, to cut down the trees!" said Matsu, jokingly.

Matsu never talked about the fighting in Wakamatsu. The war was over, but many people died there. Matsu's samurai family had been loyal to the daimyo's shogun family for hundreds of years. Now Matsu was here in America, and Okei wondered if any of his relatives had survived. *Not knowing,* she thought. *Not knowing is how it will always be for him.* And she understood his pain.

Matsu's voice became more serious. "Henry, as a samurai I was trained to protect Lord Matsudaira and those he instructed me to protect. I would die before I would let harm come to the Schnell family – or to Okei."

As Okei listened to his words and heard the strength of his voice when he vowed to protect her, she felt warmth come into her heart. It was a nice feeling.

Henry appeared to ponder Matsu's words, then turned to Okei and smiled. "Okei, will you dance tonight?" He imitated Okei's dance as he asked the question, and that made his two friends laugh.

"Oh, yes!" she said cheerfully.

"She is still weak, but this is her way to thank your family," said Matsu, talking slowly. "Okei has much courage. Even though she is far from home, she performs her duties here with joy and kindness."

"When you wear the *kimono,* Okei, you are beautiful," said Henry, "and when you dance, you are graceful."

Okei blushed at the word "beautiful" and smiled shyly. That was just Henry talking!

"Sometimes," Henry continued, "when you are sitting on top of the hill, I can hear you singing with the little bird. It is hard to tell which is the bird and which is you."

"Yes," said Matsu. "What a strange bird it is. It seems to watch over her and is always in the pine tree. I have seen these birds many times in Wakamatsu."

Mrs. Veerkamp poked her head out of the window and called to them. "Henry, Matsu, and Okei, if you keep talking, you will not have time to get dressed for the party!"

She pulled her head in quickly so they would not see that she still had her hair in rags. She was curling her hair for the party.

The three friends smiled and finished their work. Okei was happy and she was almost sorry that she would be going back to Japan. She would miss Henry. Matsu, of course, would go with Herr Schnell. She was sure he would, for he was family, too.

Matsu and Okei hurried home.

Chapter Twenty

Getting Dressed for the Party, May 1871

Okei pulled on the *tabi* and put on the underblouse and underskirt. She carefully combed her straight black hair into a neat bun at the back of her head. She smiled as she put on the bright red *kimono*. She held out the *obi* (long sash), and wrapped it around her waist, then tied a huge bow in the back. She tucked the red and gold fans carefully into the front of the *obi*.

The red silk *kimono* was beautiful, and when Okei wore it she felt she was beautiful, too. It had been in her family for many years. As she touched the soft silk she felt a glow of happiness, for she thought of family. Her grandmother had worn this same *kimono* when she was a young woman. Even her great-grandmother had worn this *kimono*.

Okei loved to dance and sing, so tonight would be a very special evening for her. Even more exciting was the anticipation she felt – soon she would go back to Japan with the Schnell family!

When the girls woke up from their naps, Okei dressed them in the two *kimono* she had made. Okei had even made a tiny *kimono* and *obi* for the doll.

When she stepped into the big room, Okei saw that Matsu was ready, too. His short sash was wrapped around his head. He wore *hakama* (pants), wide at the bottom, with striped *haori* (jacket). His sword was sheathed. He pulled it out part way so she could see that he had polished it until it gleamed.

His *zori* were sitting on the mat, near the front door, next to Okei's red and black *geta.* The girls giggled and laughed as Matsu pretended to dance for them.

The last thing to do was to collect the food they had prepared for the dinner. Mrs. Schnell took one final look at the plates and smiled. "Okei, I am very pleased. These dishes look so good, the food will disappear as soon as it is put on the table."

Okei knew a pleasing arrangement of food on the plate was just as important as how it tasted. She wrapped a *furoshiki* around each item – the bowl of chicken and rice-balls, the dish of pickles, and the platter of *sushi.*

Soon the Schnell family, Matsu, Okei, and the Takanos, were ready to go to the Veerkamp farm. The ladies and girls, looking quite festive in their bright *kimono,* were lifted into the wagon. When everyone was settled, Herr Schnell flicked the reins and off they went.

—*Chapter Twenty One*—

The Sayonara Party, May 1871

*T*here were many families in the yard, talking, laughing, children playing, when the Schnell group arrived. Mrs. Veerkamp came over and greeted Herr and Mrs. Schnell and the others, then turned to Okei, smiled, and said, *"Konbanwa"* (good evening), *Okei.*

"Konbanwa, Mrs. Veerkamp-san." Okei bowed in greeting and offered the food they had brought. *"Dozo"* (please).

"Thank you," said Mrs. Veerkamp as she took one of the *furoshiki*-wrapped dishes and led her guests to the tables.

Okei saw the food on the big table – platters and bowls still covered with cloths or lids – and she knew some of the dishes would contain corn relish, baked beans, fried chicken, and cakes. She was reminded of the first time they had brought Japanese food to a picnic. The Californians were afraid to taste it. None of them had ever seen Japanese food before, and it looked funny to them. But they did try it and they liked most of it, especially *yakitori,* chicken dipped in soy sauce. Then she laughed at herself, for she remembered her first taste of milk and she did not like it at all. Bread tasted odd at first, too, but now it tasted good.

Mrs. Schnell smiled as she watched her friends enjoying the food she had brought. "How funny our neighbors are," she had once said. "They do not like *sushi!"* Mrs. Schnell had brought the seaweed-wrapped rice, raw fish, and vegetables to a previous party, and the Californians had been hesitant to try it.

Herr Schnell's favorite American food was apple pie, so Mrs. Veerkamp had taught Mrs. Schnell how to make it. She had also taught her friend how to make sourdough bread, and Mrs. Veerkamp had been heard to say that Mrs. Schnell's sourdough bread was at least equal to the county's best.

When it was time for the entertainment, Mr. Veerkamp put three stools in front of the tables, took his fiddle out of its case and sat on one of the stools. Henry brought his harmonica out of his pocket while his brother Frank grabbed a couple of spoons. Each of the boys sat on a stool and practiced for a few minutes. Somebody called out to Mr. Veerkamp, "How about playing 'She'll Be Coming 'Round The Mountain'!" The boys nodded to their father, and they all started playing their instruments, Frank clicking the spoons in a most resounding fashion on his knee. Soon everyone was singing and clapping and having a good time.

Okei could not sing the songs yet but she enjoyed listening and watching. It had seemed strange at first to hear the country music, to see the women holding their skirts up as they danced, swinging around with their partners, feet quick-stepping. Everyone danced, even the children.

When it was Okei's turn to entertain, she stood in front of the guests, removed the folded fans from her *obi* and opened them. With slightly bended knees and very small steps she danced as she sang a traditional folk song. Mrs. Schnell played the *samisen*.

Okei swayed and turned gracefully, her face showing deep feelings of sadness then joy, hands in perfect symmetry with turns, altogether as one. She bent low and swayed back and forth and around, slowly, wide turns, stretching fans out – her story, sickness and sorrow. She rapidly opened and closed the fans, making them flutter quickly, up and down –

happiness. Finally she brought them to the front, lowered her face, and closed the fans. She tucked them back into her *obi*. Her dance was over.

Okei's heart was beating fast. She was pleased when her friends clapped in appreciation.

Now, Matsu stood in front of the group. He stood perfectly straight, legs slightly parted. Here was a samurai! He held his gleaming *katana* in front of him, bowed, then swiftly and surely brought the sword up and around. It sang as he pulled it through the air, faster and faster, again and again. He stepped forward and back, to the side and back, the sword flying up and down and around. How powerful he was! How fast he moved! Then he stopped, sheathed his sword, and bowed to the audience. There was much clapping and much praise for this performer, also.

"How strong he is!" thought Okei, filled with pride that he was her friend.

When it was time to say goodbye, the mood changed. The Schnell group was very somber and so were all the Gold

Hill neighbors. They wished the Schnells a safe journey. The promise of success for the colony was in jeopardy if Herr Schnell did not bring back more plants and money. The neighbors were still waving goodbye as the wagon pulled away from the Veerkamp farmhouse.

Okei did not feel sad. Soon she would be leaving for Japan with Herr Schnell and his family and she hoped she would see her own family again. She yearned to find news of them or, even better, to see them.

Chapter Twenty Two

Sad News, May 1871

*T*he next morning brought promise of a beautiful spring day – birds singing, sun shining. Okei was cheerfully looking forward to the trip home . . . until she saw Mrs. Schnell. Tears glistened in Mrs. Schnell's eyes, and the words to come were not those Okei expected to hear this morning.

"Okei," said Mrs. Schnell, "I am very sorry. We will not be taking you home with us. Schnell-san thinks you are too ill to travel." She reached for Okei's hands and held them gently in her own. "Matsu will remain here with you."

Okei was speechless. *I am not going home? Schnell-san thinks I am too ill? I am not sick! I have been improving every day. I am tired but I am not sick!* What could she do? She could not beg them to take her with them.

She reached up, touched the little whistle at her neck, and thought of Father. She tried desperately to calm herself. She looked at Mrs. Schnell and said quietly, "May I please tell Frances-chan and Mary-chan I will not be going with them?" Mrs. Schnell nodded and turned away.

It would be another hour at least before the girls woke up, so Okei climbed to the top of her hill. She kneeled down and looked to the west, toward Japan. Her heart ached, and she did not understand why Herr Schnell would not take her home. *Am I not part of their family? Am I only a nanny, after all, with no family of my own?* She rocked slowly back and forth, trying very hard not to cry, but she could not hold the tears back. For a long time she sobbed until finally there were no more tears left.

Okei knew she could not stay on the hill forever. Frustrated, she spoke out loud, "Why are they going home without me?" She stopped rocking and buried her head in her arms. "Why are they leaving me here? Mother! Father!" she called out. "I do not want to be sick. I want to go home."

"Cheep-cheep-cheep! Cheeaa! Cheeaa!" sang the little red finch. Okei looked at him and sighed. "I see you, my friend. Will you go home without me, too?"

"Cheeaa! Cheeaa!" was all he said as he shook himself all over and fluffed up his feathers.

Okei tried to smile, but there was no smile in her heart. She reached out and picked up two red feathers that had floated to the ground. "Thank you, little bird. I cannot cheer up, but I will be honorable."

Okei stood and slowly started to walk down the hill. The next few hours would not be easy, but somehow she would manage. She stumbled and fell, landing on her knees. Before she pulled herself up she felt a sliver of ice go from her head to her toes as a chilling thought surfaced. *They are not coming back!* Then she argued with herself. *But Schnell-okusan said she would come back, and Schnell-san promised the workers he would return, and he has never lied to them. They could be back in three months, maybe sooner. I know they will return.*

She touched the little whistle hanging on her neck. She blew into it, small quick bursts, then stronger. She did not want to wait. She wanted to go home now, with the Schnells! "Do you hear me, Father?" She blew again. "I want to come home! Help me, Father! Please!" She blew the whistle once more, then slowly stood up and headed back to the house. It would not be easy to say goodbye to the girls.

Chapter Twenty Three

Saying Goodbye, May 1871

*I*t was time for the Schnells to leave. Okei forced herself to smile as she went into the girls' room.

"*Ohayo gozaimasu,* Frances-chan and Mary-chan."

"*Ohayo go . . .,*" said Frances. Then she reached up to Okei's face and brushed a finger along her cheek where a tear had escaped. She looked into Okei's eyes and said softly, "Okei?"

"It is all right, Frances-chan. I will not be able to go with you today."

"No, Okei. You must come with us!" said Frances.

Okei tried to smile as she took two red origami birds out of her sleeve and gave them to the girls. "Here is a gift for each of you, for you to remember me. Look closely at the paper birds. The little finch has given you a gift, too. Do you recognize the feather next to the bird's heart?" The girls nodded their heads. "I am not well enough to go with you, but I will wait here until you return. I love you both so much and I will miss you."

Mary clung to Okei, first looking at Frances, then at her nanny, and then she started to cry. Okei hugged both girls, trying to keep sad thoughts away. She mustered all her strength, took the girls' hands, and led them outside. It was time to go.

Mrs. Schnell looked sad also. She had already said goodbye to Okei, and now there was nothing more to say.

Kuninosuke would be in charge of the farm – Herr Schnell had announced to the colonists this would be so.

Herr Schnell stood by the wagon, waiting for his family. He looked at all of the Japanese workers who were there to see him off, hope in their eyes. He spoke slowly, and not in his usual loud voice. "I will come back," he promised. "Before three months have passed, I will be standing in this yard again. I will not say *sayonara* for I will return as soon as I can."

His voice shook and he did not continue. He turned to his wife. "Jou-san, we must leave now." He helped her climb into the wagon, took the girls from Okei, and lifted them into the back of the wagon. He climbed up onto the buckboard, looked straight ahead, and picked up the reins.

"Papa-san, wait!" said Frances. She held her doll out to Okei and said, "Okei, please, this is my gift for you. I love you, Okei."

As Herr Schnell drove away from the farmhouse, the girls called out. "Okei, we love you!" They called again and again until they disappeared around the curve.

Okei watched the wagon leave, taking with it the most important people in her life. "I love you, too," she whispered. She held the little doll close to her heart and tears came. Matsu stood beside her, Matsu the samurai, strong and dependable, who could do nothing to help her now.

They were still standing in front of the house when a wagon pulled up. At first Okei thought it was Herr Schnell, but it was only Henry.

"Hey, you two," he called out as he reined in the horse. "My mother almost had a heart attack when she saw Herr

Schnell go past our house. She saw that you weren't in the wagon, Okei, and she told me to fetch you both. I'm taking you home, to our house."

Okei just stared at him. She was exhausted and confused. What was he saying? So much had happened today, so much sadness. She did not understand him.

"Come on, Okei. Mother's got the soup on the stove and the pies are in the oven. Hurry up, Matsu, before my brothers get to them."

Matsu looked at Okei and smiled. "Come, Okei. Henry's mother wants us to stay with them until Schnell-san returns. She will not take no for an answer."

They went into the house to collect their belongings. Matsu helped Okei climb into the wagon. She could hardly see where she was going; she was blinded by the steady flow of tears, and she did nothing to stop them. When the three friends were finally settled, Henry flicked the reins, and the horse slowly pulled the wagon away from the Wakamatsu Tea and Silk Farm.

Chapter Twenty Four

A New Home, Veerkamp Farm, May 1871

The sun was already shining the next morning when Okei awoke to the aroma of freshly baked bread. She dressed quickly. She should have been up earlier! She should be helping Mrs. Veerkamp make breakfast for her family. She was not in the habit of sleeping late.

"Good morning, Okei," said Mrs. Veerkamp, smiling, as Okei hurried into the kitchen. She was rolling out pie dough, and the bread that smelled so good was still baking in the oven.

"Good morning, Mrs. Veerkamp-san." Okei always pronounced each syllable carefully, trying to make the words sound right. English words were difficult. She looked around to see what she could do to help. The baby, Louis, was asleep in the cradle. She saw apples on the counter so she peeled and sliced them and had them ready for the pie shells before the rest of the family came into the kitchen.

They were a noisy bunch. There was much talking and laughing among Henry, Frank, William, Egbert, Barthold, and their father. This morning they were having eggs, fried potatoes, bacon, and freshly baked bread – everything heaped onto large platters and passed around at the table. The entire family sat at the large table, Matsu also. The kitchen was quiet only when they all trooped out in their heavy boots to do their chores.

Okei cleared the table and washed the dishes, so many

plates, glasses, pots, and pans. Mrs. Veerkamp removed the pies from the oven and set them out to cool. Then they sat down for a cup of tea. Today Okei would learn what her chores would be. She knew she would help Mrs. Veerkamp inside the house and also help take care of Louis. Matsu would help with outside chores. There was much work to do in a large family and on such a large farm. Matsu and Okei both agreed they wanted to work hard so they would not be a burden to the Veerkamps. In her own mind, Okei honored her parents by working diligently.

Later that week a gentleman arrived on horseback and had a lengthy talk with Mr. Veerkamp. After the man left, Mr. Veerkamp came slowly up the stairs, onto the porch, and sat down in a chair opposite his wife.

"How strange," he uttered as he looked out toward the Wakamatsu Farm, where some of the Japanese gardeners were still working in the fields. Henry and Matsu, standing nearby, waited silently. Mrs. Veerkamp and Okei stopped snapping green beans.

"It appears," said Mr. Veerkamp, "that Herr Schnell has no intention of returning to Gold Hill. He did not make payments on the farm, and it has reverted back to the county." He pulled his eyes away from the fields and looked at his wife. "Louisa, I have agreed to purchase it."

Matsu turned to Okei and repeated Mr. Veerkamp's solemn announcement. Okei stared at Mr. Veerkamp, her heart churning, mind spinning. She looked at Matsu, not believing what she had just heard. He nodded his head, yes. Her hands shook violently as she started snapping beans again. The only sound that could be heard was her frantic snap, snap, snapping. Mrs. Veerkamp reached over and gently held Okei's hands until she stopped shaking and was able to breathe normally again.

"Well," said Mrs. Veerkamp, her eyes sparkling kindly as she looked at Okei. "We have just become one very large family."

Chapter Twenty Five

The Final Days,
June, July, August 1871

*T*he days went by slowly after Herr Schnell's departure. During the first month Okei found it difficult to believe he would not return. She struggled with feelings of desertion but tried very hard not to let sadness show. She loved taking care of Louis, now two months old. His baby laughter made her laugh, too. Sometimes Mrs. Veerkamp would put her arms around Okei and Louis, hugging them both, and Okei could feel the love flowing around her.

Mrs. Veerkamp taught her how to do needlework and how to cook. She learned quickly. She usually hummed quietly while she worked. One day she overheard Mrs. Veerkamp say to her husband, "I like having a girl in my family."

Okei liked being part of this family, too, and she enjoyed working with Mrs. Veerkamp. They laughed together when Mrs. Veerkamp tried to teach Okei how to speak English. She could not speak it very well, even though she practiced often. She could understand it much better than she could speak it.

Mrs. Veerkamp and Okei always had tea in the afternoon, in the kitchen. Okei prepared the tea while Mrs. Veerkamp fed Louis. Today was another dry day, no rain, but this farm had wells that were still giving water, enough for field plants and farmhouse.

Okei poured the tea. She sat at the table with her hands folded tightly around the hot cup, and said quietly, "Mrs. Veerkamp-san, I think of my mother now."

Mrs. Veerkamp was just starting to take her first sip of tea. Her hand stopped in mid air. She placed the cup back on the table, looked directly at Okei, and said gently, "Please, Okei, tell me about your parents. I know they must love you very much."

Okei sighed. She had wanted so badly to talk about her family but there was never the opportunity. Wasn't she just the nanny? Now Mrs. Veerkamp was willing to listen, so Okei began to share memories, good memories with her, in halting English mixed with Japanese words. She talked about the old *keyaki* tree in the yard, her trips to the market, helping Mother in the garden, and when she talked of Father she remembered his sternness and also his love. She showed Mrs. Veerkamp the whistle he had made. The memories surprisingly brought smiles and laughter along with some sadness.

By the second month Okei did not feel homesick anymore. She often sang while she worked, and she tried to teach the younger boys how to sing her songs. No matter how hard they tried, they could not pronounce the words. Still they always asked her to sing.

Okei visited the top of the hill every day at sunset. She kneeled on her quilt and looked out toward the mountains, the ones that reminded her of Mount Seaburi near her home in Wakamatsu, Japan. She was at peace. Sometimes, though, when she closed her eyes, she could almost see a wagon coming up the road with two little girls leaning over the sides, laughing and waving and then she felt a pang of remorse.

There was very little work being done on the Wakamatsu Tea and Silk Farm. Kuninosuke visited Matsu and Okei often and he offered news that was not good. Many workers were leaving the farm in search of other jobs. Supplies were almost gone, and food was scarce, so Kuninosuke had sold some of the animals to local farmers. He shared the proceeds with the other workers. Some of them talked about going back to Japan as soon as they could earn enough money. They no longer expected Herr Schnell to return.

Sundays were restful days on the farm. Nights were longer now, sun setting later in the sky. On Sundays, Matsu hiked up the hill with Okei, carrying a picnic basket. They would share a meal Mrs. Veerkamp had prepared for them, and they would kneel together on the quilt, sometimes looking at each other and sometimes looking past the hilltops toward their old home in Japan. Okei was content. She enjoyed time spent alone with Matsu and she permitted herself to dream of future happiness.

At the end of three months, Okei began to feel tired and weak again. Her treks up the hill became a bit more difficult and she walked slower. Then her illness came back with a vengeance, attacking her body from the inside. Her beautiful black hair became limp, with no shine to it. She could not walk with Matsu. She could not laugh with him. The pain took all other thoughts away. She could smile, though. Always she smiled at him.

The Gold Hill doctor came to see her, to examine her. He did bring flowers and he did hide them behind his back, but when he came into the room he brought them out slowly, and he did not say, "Surprise!" He became quiet, and when he opened his new medicine case he seemed to find nothing in there that could cure her. The doctor brought medicine to help with the pain. He did not bring hope.

After the doctor left, Okei said, "Matsu-san, I am not going to get better, am I?" She looked at him, begging him to tell her she was wrong. He did not answer, and she realized that he could not. The answer was already in his eyes.

"Matsu-san," she said a few days later, "I do not want to be a burden, but I do want to climb my hill. Will you help me?" She spent all her time in bed now.

Matsu, the samurai, the warrior, bowed low and spoke with fervor and humor in his voice. "I would carry you to the top of a mountain and back a hundred times, no a thousand times, if only you should ask, for you are no burden at all." The nanny and the samurai had always been very good at pretending.

Matsu carried Okei up the hill every evening when his chores were done. They kneeled together on the knoll listening to the little bird's cheerful melodies. The samurai held her, his arms wrapped gently around her, so she could look toward her beloved Japan. Sometimes he hummed to her, his voice mingling with the bird's melody.

One day Okei was so ill she could barely talk. Mrs. Veerkamp held her in her arms and sang to her. Okei grasped her hand and whispered, *"Arigato."* She remembered the many good things this kind lady had done for her. Mrs. Veerkamp smoothed Okei's hair back as she lowered her down on the bed. She placed her hands gently on each side of Okei's face, leaned close and said, "You have been a joy to us, Okei. You have been like a daughter to me." She brushed her hands along Okei's cheeks, no longer smooth and young, kissed her one last time, and quietly left the room.

Soon Henry came in to say goodbye. He sat beside her but words did not come. Okei smiled at him, this boy who was her age, first her friend, then her 'brother.' She felt old and tired. Was she really only nineteen years old?

Later Matsu kneeled down beside her bed. Okei looked at him and tried to reach out to touch his face. She felt the familiar warmth fill her heart. She loved being with him. She was safe in his arms. Still, the desire to go home, to Japan, was strong.

"Matsu-san, will you carry me to the top of my hill one more time?"

Matsu wrapped the quilt around her, picked her up and carried her across the field and up the hill. The sun was beginning to set and the sky was a vivid red, soon turning to gold, with bright streaks of light fanning out as the sun slid behind the horizon.

He very carefully kneeled down and held her on his lap. They looked at the beautiful sunset together.

After awhile, Okei asked, "Matsu-san, why did Schnell-san leave and why has he not returned?"

"I do not know, Okei. I believe he wanted to come back. He did not want the colony to fail. Do you remember how happy he was when the plants were healthy and growing? We were all happy then." He looked directly into her eyes. "I promise you, Okei, that I will never leave you."

"Oh, Matsu-san! *Arigato.*" She paused, taking short, shallow breaths, then reached up to touch his face. "What is that on your cheek? A samurai does not shed tears."

He gently covered her hand with his. "Why must I not shed tears? First I think of happiness and what might have been. Then I am sad because I cannot help you. Okei-san, I am losing you today!"

"Oh, Matsu-san, how can I leave you? I do not want to go!"

They knelt together, not talking, just kneeling – tears falling, mingling into one steady stream.

Finally Okei said, "Matsu-san, please sing to me."

"Okei-san, I cannot sing now."

"I am too tired to talk," she whispered, "but I can hear you. Please?"

He rested his head gently on hers and he sang, not loudly. Okei closed her eyes and was at peace as she listened to the beautiful music that would take her home.

The End

─Okei's Lullaby─

Words by M. Shimizu
Music by I. Tone

NE — N NE — N O KO— RO RI   I KO KU NO   O KA DE

O KE — I JU — SI — — TI   A — — — NA ZE NA I TA

O — KU NI   NA MA RI NO YO   KO MO RI U TA   KO MO RI U TA

U TA I NA GA RA MO   SA — — — NA ZE NA I TA   NA ZE NA I TA

Refrain of rock-a-bye, heard in far away land,
Okei, just seventeen, why did she cry?
As she quietly sang the Lullaby
Of her native land, why did she cry?

Refrain of rock-a-bye, distant clouds swept by,
In the lonely sunset, her heart searched afar,
Only in her dreams could she return home,
Toward her beloved Aizu, she watched the stars.

The song of rock-a-bye, she sang as she cried,
Gentle Okei, longing and waiting in vain,
As winter fled and spring had arrived,
For glad tidings from home, which never came.

(Interpretation of Okei's Lullaby) Henry Taketa

120

—Epilogue—

Henry Veerkamp was just one year older than Okei. At the age of seventy-five he was quoted as saying, "Okei-san was a nice girl, and when she wore a Japanese kimono she was really beautiful. She couldn't speak English very much, but was bright, and soon learned needlework and cooking from Mother, who was very fond of her." (Phillip Veerkamp's website)

Okei died in August of 1871 and was buried on the top of a small hill in Gold Hill, California. She was 19 years old. The samurai, Matsunosuke Sakurai (Matsu), purchased Okei's tombstone and had one side engraved in Japanese and the other side in English: "In Memory of Okei, Died 1871, Age 19 Years, a Japanese Girl."(Phillip Veerkamp's website)

John Henry Schnell, the leader of a group of colonists from Wakamatsu, Japan, returned to Japan in 1871 and did not come back to Gold Hill. The tea-gardeners stayed on the farm for a while but left when they realized Schnell was not coming back. Many of them found jobs in Sacramento or other areas of California. They were capable and good workers and some of them eventually earned enough money to return to Japan.

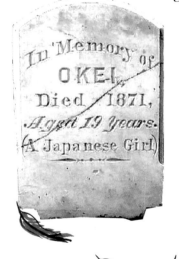

Masumizu Kuninosuke (Kuni), the carpenter, moved to Sacramento, married Carrie Wilson, became a fisherman, a farmer, an interpreter, and owned a fish shop. He moved to Colusa, California, and was buried there. His descendents live in California and are the only known descendants of the Wakamatsu Colony. He was twenty years old when he came to America.

In late 1867 the Chosu and Satsuma clans took control of the imperial court in Kyoto and designated themselves as imperial forces. They also took control of the thirteen-year-old emperor, Meiji. In October 1868 they marched to the castle town of Wakamatsu, the capital of Aizu, and after heavy fighting, defeated Matsudaira Katamori, the last Tokugawa feudal lord of Japan. The daimyo surrendered the castle on November 5, 1868.

The period 1868 to 1869 was a period of destruction and starvation for the people of Aizu. Many of them migrated north to Tohoku and Hokkaido and other parts of Japan. Three small groups went to America with Herr Schnell. This was the end of 268 years of Tokugawa rule and the beginning of the Meiji Restoration. For the members of the Wakamatsu Tea and Silk Farm Colony there would be no Wakamatsu to go home to, no families and no buildings. The Chosu/Satsuma soldiers burned the entire town in November 1868. The castle was demolished in 1874.

Matsudaira Katamori, the daimyo (feudal lord) of Aizu, was imprisoned in a monastery for a short time and was pardoned the following year. He became a Shinto priest and served for many years as chief priest at Toshogu Shrine in Nikko, the mausoleum of the founder of the Tokugawa Shogunate. He married and had five sons after the castle fell. He died in 1893 at the age of 58.

John Henry Schnell came to Japan in 1861. By 1867 he had become a confidant of Lord Matsudaira Katamori and was permitted to marry a Japanese girl, Jou, from a samurai family. He was given samurai status, a house in Wakamatsu, and a monthly stipend. His samurai name was Hiramatsu. No record has been

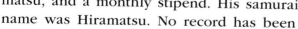

found of John Henry Schnell returning to Japan. It is not known where the family went when they left Gold Hill, although records do show that Eduard Schnell, John's brother, was in Yokohama during and after the Boshin Civil War. The brothers were actually from Germany. John Henry Schnell was thirty-four years old when he brought his wife and daughter and other members of the Wakamatsu Tea and Silk Farm Colony to America in 1869. He brought a total of three groups of people, from 1869 to 1870, twenty-five to thirty people altogether.

The hollyhock emblem on a silk banner, a bowl and a tanto dagger led researchers to the Tokugawa Daimyo of Wakamatsu, Lord Matsudaira Katamori. It is believed the relics were left behind as collateral. The dagger, which dates back to the year 1354, was that of a woman, so it possibly belonged to Jou Schnell.

In 2001 the Veerkamp family donated the banner and dagger to Marshall Gold Discovery State Historic Park in Coloma, three miles from the colony site. The Veerkamp family had preserved the Japanese relics for over 130 years. Francis and Louisa Veerkamp were successful and highly respected farmers in El Dorado County. Phillip Veerkamp (great-grandson) and Cindy Akin (great-great-granddaughter) of Francis and Louisa Veerkamp are active perservers and conveyors of the family history.

Matsunosuke Sakurai (Matsu) worked for the Veerkamps for many years and became the manager of all of Henry Veerkamp's agricultural enterprises. Ada Veerkamp Rose, Henry's niece, grew up hearing stories about the Japanese girl who, for a short time, was part of her family. She remembered that her grandfather's nickname for Matsunosuke was Motts. At age ninety-five she recounted that her grandfather and Motts had great respect for each other.

Matsunosuke died February 23, 1901 and was buried in the Vineyard Cemetery in Coloma in an unmarked grave. He is described as being of middle age when he came to America.

Other Japanese had come to America, but this was the first

organized emigration of a group of Japanese to America. Okei was the first Japanese woman of record to be buried in America. Mary Schnell was the first child of a Japanese parent to be born in America.

The PMSS China was one of the last four wooden side-wheelers built in America. It was built in 1867. From 1868 to 1871 it was regularly sailing from Honk Kong to Yokohama to San Francisco and back.

The Alameda was only one of many side-wheelers on the Sacramento River from 1866 to 1880. Our great-grandfather Commodore Herman Martin Alpen owned the Alameda and two other boats. It is not known which boat the Schnell group actually took. There were many boats that were lost on the river, some because their captains pushed them too hard and the boilers exploded. Commodore Alpen did rescue survivors of a sinking vessel – acknowledgment date, January 13, 1873.

In the 1960s, in Japan, on Mount Seaburi overlooking Aizu-Wakamatsu, a monument was dedicated to the Wakamatsu Colony. The center of this monument is an exact replica of Okei's headstone in Gold Hill, California. The old Wakamatsu is now called Aizu-Wakamatsu.

In 1969 a monument was erected at Gold Trail Elementary School in Gold Hill, California in recognition of the centennial anniversary of the founding of the colony. It is listed as California Registered Historical Landmark Number 815. Okei's gravesite sits on the hill overlooking Gold Trail Elementary School.

—Glossary—

Aizu *(ah-ee-zoo)* - Tokugawa domain on Island of Honshu, Japan.

Arigato *(ah-ree-gah-tohh)* - Thank you.

Bamboo whistle - Small whistle made from bamboo plant, native to Wakamatsu, Japan.

Bento box - Box for holding meals; with separate sections; often wrapped in a furoshiki.

Boshin Civil War - A war in Japan that ended the rule of the Tokugawa family in 1868 and led into the Meiji Restoration.

Chamber pot - Pot placed under bed for nighttime use.

Chopsticks - Eating utensils.

Chosu - Domain in southern Japan.

Coloma - Town in Northern California where gold was discovered in 1848.

Daimyo *(dah-eem-yoh)* - Regional feudal lord. Lord Matsudaira was the daimyo of Aizu.

Dozo *(doh- zoh)* - Please.

Furoshiki (foo-roh-shee-kee) - Square cloth of any size.

Futon *(foo-tahn)* - Long, sectioned pad used as bed; can be folded when not being used.

Geta *(geh-tah)* - Wooden clogs.

Gig - Small rowing boat attached to large ship.

Gold Hill - City near Coloma in Northern California.

Gold Hill Ditch - Creek running alongside Graner farm.

Graner Farm - Purchased by Herr Schnell. Renamed Wakamatsu Tea and Silk Colony.

Hai *(Hah-ee)* - Yes. A form of expression.

Herr - German title similar to mister.

Imperial Forces - Self-designated name of Chosu and Satsuma samurai after they took control of Imperial Palace in Kyoto in 1867.

Jou *(joh)* - Jou Schnell, Japanese wife of John Henry Schnell.

Louisa *(loo-ee-zah)* - Mrs. Veerkamp

Katana *(kah-tah-nah)* - Samarai long sword. Approximately three feet long.

Keyaki tree *(kay-yah-kee)* - Tree native to Japan. A keyaki tree still grows in Gold Hill.

Kimono *(kee-moh-noh)* - Silk full-length robe with wide sleeves and wide sash (obi). I have used the Japanese form of kimono; there is no 's' added for plural.

Koi *(koy)* - Carp, fish.

Konbanwa *(kohn-bahn-wah)* - Good evening.

Konnichiwa *(kohn-nee-chee-wah)* - Good afternoon.

Matsu *(maht-soo)* - Shortened name of the samurai from Wakamatsu.

Matsu-san *(maht-soo-sahn)* - Honorific name.

Misoshiru *(mee-soh-shee-roo)* - Soybean-paste soup.

Niigata *(nee-gah-tah)* - Port city northwest of Wakamatsu on Sea of Japan

Obi *(oh-bee)* - Wide sash wrapped around kimono, large knot or bow at back.

Ohayo gozaimasu *(oh-hah-yohh goh-zah-ee-mahs)* - Good morning.

Okei *(Oh-kay)* - Japanese girl's name.

Okei-chan *(Oh-kay-chahn)* - Parent or family name for Okei.

Origami *(oh-ree-gah-mee)* - Art of paper folding.

PMSS China - One of the four largest wooden side-wheeler steamships running from Hong Kong to Yokohama to San Francisco 1867 to 1879.

Paddle-wheel - Large wooden wheel on sides of ship or boat (side-wheeler) or at back of ship or boat (stern-wheeler).

Porthole - Round window in boat.

Queue *(kyoo)* - Samurai hair style; hair pulled back and tied at top/back of head.

Red Crossbill - Red bird with crossed bill; of the finch family; eats pine cone seeds.

Sacramento - Capital city of California.

Sacramento River - River running north to south in California.

Saloon - Large room on boat or ship; social room.

Samisen *(sah-mih-sen)* - Three-stringed Japanese square-shaped lute.

Samurai *(sah-moo-rah-ee)* - Professional warriors of Japan for 680 years (1188 to 1868).

San *(sahn)* - Honorific addition to a name.

San Francisco - Large port city in northern California.

Satsuma *(saht-soo-mah)* - Domain or province in southern Japan.

Sayonara *(sah-yohh-nah-rah)* - Goodbye.

Schnell-okusan *(schnell-oh-koo-sahn)* - Honorific name for wife of Herr Schnell.

Schnell-san *(schnell-sahn)* - Honorific name for Herr Schnell.

Shoji *(show-gee)* - Sliding door.

Side-wheeler - Ship or boat with paddle-wheel on both sides of boat.

Stern-wheeler - Ship or boat with paddle-wheel at end of boat.

Steamship - Large ocean sailing vessel, powered by steam formed by burning coal to turn large paddle-wheels.

Sushi *(soo-shee)* - Popular Japanese food. Seaweed wrapped rice, fish and vegetables.

Tabi *(tah-bee)* - Socks; separation between big toe and remaining toes; worn with geta or sandals.

Tadaima *(tah-dah-ee-mah)* - Greeting; loose translation - "I'm home!"

Tatami *(tah-tah-mee)* - Woven straw mats.

Tokugawa *(toh-koo-gah-wah)* - Ruling family of Japan from 1603-1868.

Tsuruga Castle - Tokugawa castle of Aizu in Wakamatsu.

Wakamatsu *(wah-kah-maht-soo)* - Castle town of Aizu domain.

Wakizashi *(wah-kee-zah-shee)* - Samurai short sword; approximately two feet long.

Yokohama *(yoh-koh-hah-mah)* - Port city, south of Wakamatsu, on Tokyo Bay near the Pacific Ocean.

Yukata *(yoo-kah-tah)* - Cotton kimono.

—Bibliography—

BOOKS

Chamberlain, Basil Hall. *Japanese Things*, 1904
Chandler, Robert J. and Potash, Stephen J. *Gold, Silk, Pioneers & Mail*, 2007
Dunn, Charles J. *Everyday Life in Traditional Japan*, 1969
Hanley, Susan B. *Everyday Things in Premodern Japan*, 1997
Hornor, Ric & Jody. *The Golden Corridor*, 2005
Kemble, John Haskell. *Side-Wheelers Across the Pacific*, 1942
Kure, Mitsuo. *Samurai, An Illustrated History*, 2002
MacMullen, Jerry. *Paddle-Wheel Days in California*, 1944
Maeda, Wayne. *Changing Dreams and Treasured Memories*, 2000
Maraini, Fosco. *Meeting with Japan*
Sadler, A.L. *The Japanese Tea Ceremony*, 2008
Saga, Dr. Junichi. *Memories of Silk and Straw*, 1987
Sioli, Paolo. *Historical Souvenir of El Dorado County, California*, 1998, (1883)
Stahncke, Holmer. *The Brothers Schnell and the Civil War in North Japan*, 1986 translated by Paul F. C. Mueller, 2004
Starns, Jean E. *Gold Hill: Bonds of Time, Families & Land*, 1993
Turnbull, Stephen. *The Book of the Samurai, The Warrior Class of Japan*, 1982
Van Sant, John E. *Pacific Pioneers*, 2000
Yohalem, Betty. *I Remember*, 1997

BOOKLETS

Flynn, Halmar Forrest. *El Dorado Sketches*. Ill by George Mathis, 1973
Japanese American Citizens League. *Wakamatsu Colony Centennial*, 1969
Taketa, Henry. *The Centennial Year*, 1969

LIBRARIES

Bancroft Library, Berkeley, California
California State Library, Sacramento, California
East Asiatic Library, Berkeley, California
East Asian Library, Berkeley, California
El Dorado County Library, Placerville, California
Marshall Gold Discovery Park Library, Coloma, California

MAGAZINES AND PERIODICALS

California Historian, Vol. 38, No. 3. 1992. *HEARD IN FAR-AWAY LAND* by Henry Taketa
Sierra Heritage Magazine, *The Legend of Okei*, by Bill Dillinger. Photos by Henry Taketa

MAPS AND PHOTOGRAPHS

Stephen J. and Jeremy W. Potash for use of the rare original 1867 lithograph of the SS China (I) by Endicott & Company, New York, from their Pacific Mail Steamship Collection.
Elena DeLacy, Cartographer, Courtesy of American River Conservancy, for combining the Map of Japan and the 1867 lithograph of the Pacific Mail steamer China (from the Stephen J. and Jeremy W. Potash Pacific Mail Steamship Collection) – Shows land and sea routes.
For use of the historical map of river and land routes from San Francisco to Gold Hill. Courtesy of El Dorado County Historical Museum, Placerville, CA. Show townships, etc.
Graner House Photography, Phillip Veerkamp, May 2000

MUSEUMS AND GOVERNMENT AGENCIES

El Dorado County Department of Transportation, Placerville, California, Kris Payne
El Dorado County Surveyor's Department, Placerville, California, Karen Hyder
El Dorado County Historical Museum, Placerville, California
National Archives, San Bruno, California
San Francisco Maritime National Historical Park, San Francisco
Steinhart Aquarium Natural History Museum, San Francisco

NEWSPAPERS

Georgetown Gazette, California
Mainichi Daily News, Japan
Mountain Democrat, California
Pacific Historian, University of Pacific, California
Sacramento Daily Union, California
San Francisco Bulletin, California
San Francisco Chronicle, California
San Francisco Daily Alta, California
Yomiuri Japan News, Japan

RECORDS

State of California, County of El Dorado. *Indenture.* Charles M. Graner/J. Henry Schnell, 6/18/1869.
El Dorado County 1870 Census.
Report of U.S. Surveyor General for California. December 1870.
State of California, County of El Dorado. *Decree of Foreclosure,* 12/7/1870.
Bill passed through congress, not to interfere with colony. April 1871.
El Dorado County Records. *J.H. Schnell to the County of El Dorado,* 1 May 1871.
Congressional Record. House of Representatives. *JACL Celebrates Centennial of Wakamatsu Tea And Silk Colony At Gold Hill, California.* Vol. 115 No. 74 May, 1969.

RESEARCH PAPERS

Akin, Cindy. *Veerkamp Family Historic Relationship to the Wakamatsu Silk and Tea Colony.*
Mueller, Paul. *Research of the Brothers Schnell,* 2004-2006.
Nakatani, Soichi. Unpublished papers, notes, and tape.
Van Sant, John. *The Wakamatsu Colony: From Aizu to Gold Hill,* May 28, 1992.
Veerkamp, Phil. Family recollections, photos, notes, website.
Sayre, Fern. *The Research Story of The Wakamatsu Colony and Okei-san,* 1967.

The Graner house and the Keyaki tree.
Phillip Veerkamp, May 2000.

Author's notes by Joan Barsotti

Okei was seventeen years old when she came to America in 1869 and only nineteen when she died in 1871. I had stated repeatedly that I would never write a chapter book and I would never write a story with an unhappy ending! I am a picture book author and I enjoy writing cheerful stories for elementary school-age children.

But, this is a local story, a true story about a girl who came to this country, probably not by choice, who worked very hard to do her best, and by so doing would honor her parents. She was a pioneer in every sense of the word.

In 1868 Japan was embroiled in a civil war. Okei's hometown was destroyed, her family's whereabouts unknown. She came to California with a group of gardeners and samurai to start a tea and silk colony. The leader of the group, John Henry Schnell, was an honorary samurai. His wife Jou was the daughter of a samurai, and Okei was the nanny for the Schnell children.

After two fairly successful years, the colony began to fail. Herr Schnell went back to Japan promising to return with more supplies. He took his wife and two daughters, but left everyone else behind, including the nanny.

This is my interpretation of Okei's story. I liked her very much. She was never able to overcome her homesickness, but she tried. She did not think she was courageous, but she was steadfast and loving. The neighbor, Louisa Veerkamp loved her like a daughter. Matsu, the samurai, cared enough to have a tombstone made for her. She was just "Okei" when she came to America, but when Henry Veerkamp was interviewed many years later, he referred to her as "Okei-san" with the honorific title.

For many years people have come to visit the gravesite, often from Japan. The gravesite is small; sits by itself atop a small hill overlooking Gold Trail School, and beyond that, thousands of miles away, Japan. Okei was never forgotten. Could it be that she was somebody special, after all? I think so. If all she did was to leave a legacy of friendship between people of two countries, then that is pretty remarkable in itself!

I hope you enjoy reading this story,
Joan Barton Barsotti

Acknowledgments by Joan Barton Barsotti, Author

There were many people who helped me write Okei's story, who provided sage advice, constant support, read multiple rewrites, corrected or redirected my efforts, and most of all were enthusiastic about this project. I would like to thank these wonderful people:

Cindy Akin and *Phil Veerkamp,*
Patty Borelli, Normadine Carpenter, Bev Cola, and *Halmar Flynn,*
Janet Cohen and *her students,*
Myrna Hanses, Laurie Edwards, Pat Monzo of *PTPI,*
Tom Fujimoto and *Sally Taketa (Mrs. Henry Taketa),*
Dr. Paul Mueller,
Stan, Susan, Suzanne, and *Stanley Sasaki,*
Jean Nakatani Yego (daughter of Soichi Nakatani),
John E. Van Sant,
Brian Hayes, Potter, etc.,
Jim Wilson, Carlton Engineering Inc.,
Naida West, Bridgehouse Books and *Alton Pryor*, Stagecoach Publishing,
Jim Grady, Marshall Gold Discovery State Historical Park,
John Hutchinson, Marshall Gold Discovery State Historical Park,
Eugene Itogawa, retired supervisor of the Office of Historic Preservation,
California Department of Parks and Recreation,
Michiko Midge Ayukawa, PhD (History), University of Victoria,
Victoria, BC, Canada,
People to People International, El Dorado County Chapter,
Joyce Hansen,
Camino Writers Group: *Jo Chandler, Madelon Phillips, Wendy Schultz, Denise Siino, Elizabeth Ward-Pabst,*
Stephen J. and *Jeremy W. Potash for use of the rare original 1867 lithograph of the SS China (I) by Endicott & Company, New York, from their Pacific Mail Steamship Collection.*

Thank you to my friends in Japan:

Haruyuki and *Shigeko Otani*, Aizuwakamatsu;
Naganori and *Masako Mukai*, Warabi;
Toshinori Iwasawa, producer of the Okei Project, A Play, Aizuwakamatsu;
Sister Cities Warabi, Japan and El Dorado County, California;
Sister Schools Higashiyama School, Aizuwakamatsu and
Gold Trail School, California.

A special thanks to:

Martha Alderson, M.A., consultant and author of Blockbuster Plots;
Sandra Williams, editor, Williams Writing, Editing & Design;
Alpen Kelley, my cousin, for her wonderful illustrations; and
my husband, *Gael Barsotti*, for his unfailing support over the last ten years.

Acknowledgments by Alpen Kelley, Illustrator

It is with sincere appreciation that I thank the following
people for their help and advice:

Gordon Whiteside for sound advice in graphics and calming;
my friends in Japan, *Haru and Shigeko Otani, and Shizuko
and Hisako Yagihashi;*
Melinda and Dave for help and wonderful hospitality;
Rio Miura for advice on Japanese costume;
my grandchildren *Leda, Kody, Alexis, and Emma,*
with hope that they will read and enjoy; and
my loving husband *Dean Kelley.*

**Books by Joan Barton Barsotti
and illustrated by Carol Mathis**

Mike And Nick And The Pumpkin Patch
Nana Gets A Cat
Christopher And Grandma on Safari
Grandmother's Bell And The Wagon Train 1849
The Little Green Frog And Other Poems
Andrew and Nana on Safari

**Books by Joan Barton Barsotti
and illustrated by Alpen Kelley**

Okei-san: The Girl From Wakamatsu
Okei-san: A Girl's Journey, Japan to California, 1868-1871

Books illustrated by Alpen Kelley

Stones To Harvest, Ayrorama Publications
Okei-san: The Girl from Wakamatsu
Okei-san: A Girl's Journey, Japan to California, 1868-1871
Various illustrations for Matrix Magazine

For more information about the books, author, and illustrator,
please go to: www.barsottibooks.com